DOORWAYS TO THE UNSEEN

6 Tales of Terror and Suspense

James Dermond

ISBN-13: 9781946038005
ISBN-10: 1946038008

Cover art by Jeff Purnawan

For the night creatures, those that infect our dreams
and those that have never visited them

CONTENTS

THE DROWNED MAN

"You made out with Joshua Barger? That is so gross. Please tell me you didn't do that." April sat in the front passenger seat, scrutinizing her friend Jessica as the two girls drove down a roadway devoid of other vehicles through densely forested areas on either side of them.

Jessica kept her eyes on the road as she steered, smiling slyly, arching her chin upward, and said, "He's really cute once you get to know him. Not at all like what people have said about him. But it was only one time anyway. I wouldn't say that it 'counted.'" Jessica continued to smile—this time with a wide grin breaking out over her plush, full-lipped mouth—while April looked away from her and out the car window, watching the bright midday sun shine over the tops of the soaring coniferous pine trees as they sped past. They were now close to Jessica's parents' summer home, which the two would have all to themselves for several weeks.

Jessica's black Labrador retriever, Marcus, sat up in the back seat from his nap and began to force his snout into April's face, nuzzling and poking her as he panted. April pushed him away. "You should keep Marcus outside as long as it's not raining. He hasn't kept his nose off me since we started the drive this morning. My only reprieve was his nap time that must have just ended. Marcus!" April pushed Marcus away from her face again. Marcus began to whine and pant more intensely, as he knew they were nearing the trio's destination; he then turned around and resumed his earlier prone position across the back seat.

Jessica held a paper-thin smile on her face but didn't respond to April. She remarked to herself that April had always been oversensitive about nearly everything: school, boys, her parents, food, things that were "gross." It was truly amazing that the girl had made it to eighteen intact. Jessica glanced over, observing April adjusting her glasses and then shifting around in the front passenger seat, unbuckling and then rebuckling her seat belt. Jessica and April's friendship had begun in middle school and then continued on into their high school years. Even though they were an unlikely pair, the girls had remained close friends, one maturing and the other staying largely the same.

Jessica had competed on the varsity swim team at their high school and continued to swim in college, developing a lithe, athletic build due to all those years of continual exertion. April was the wallflower of the duo and was working toward a degree in English literature at their university, hoping to be a teacher upon graduation. Jessica possessed an almost classic beauty, with long, light brown hair that extended over her broad shoulders, and luminous blue eyes. April appeared remarkably similar in this respect, having hair and eye colors that almost matched Jessica's, but in contrast she was frozen in a kind of permanent physical adolescence. She was very thin, and her body was nearly curveless, having grown in height during high school but otherwise appearing mostly undeveloped.

Jessica saw the unmarked entrance to the gravel road that intersected the two-lane highway and began to slow their vehicle to a crawl. Her parents' summer home was at the end of a very long, winding path that was just wide enough for a single mid-size truck and would accommodate no other traffic. After driving deliberately down the flinty road and then climbing the small hill near its low apex, Jessica stopped their car to unlock the waist-high rusted-iron gates blocking would-be intruders from parking on the property. Jessica then pulled the maroon compact car to a second stop by the toolshed in the unenclosed yard and shut off the engine.

As soon as Jessica opened one of the car's back doors, Marcus bolted out and started racing in circles around the two girls, the moment for which he had been waiting all day. Bounding around the lawn in the back and in the front of the lakefront house, Marcus then sat down facing the house near the red cedar wooden dock that extended about ten feet from the sandy shore into the pristine lake. He became very quiet, his pent-up energy now somewhat spent. Marcus tilted his head and just stared at the vacant house, making no sound, his sudden stillness mirroring that of the lake's waters.

"We've spent every summer at Lake Ultio for five years in a row, and it's always tranquil." Jessica stood next to the parked car and looked out over the circular lake's sun-spattered surface with its clear, cerulean waters as the early afternoon sunlight reflected on it. "There are neighbors on the other side of the lake, but there are some thick woods between us and their cottages. We have so much privacy here that I hate to ever have to leave it."

April, who was carrying two of her bags from the car trunk, asked, "If the neighbors want to visit, how do they stop by? Or don't they ever come to see you and your family?"

Jessica reached into the tightly packed trunk of the car and grabbed a plastic cooler by the handles. "They have to take a rowboat from the other side and park it at our dock, but neighbors don't really pay us many social calls—at least not as many as they did in past summers. Those cottages are rental units, so their summer residents are different almost every time. I can't tell you who might be living over there this tourist season."

Jessica continued to lug her cooler as she spoke to April. "I've only ever stayed here with my parents and brother, and we've never brought company. This is my first time flying solo. We used to rent one of the tiny cabins on the other side of the lake until we bought this house."

Jessica walked toward the house's cement side porch with the bulky cooler and placed it on the ground near the porch's metal railings. The one-story ranch-style house was of simple design and construction, with white aluminum siding and a red shingled roof, but it was well maintained and could easily fit into any suburban neighborhood.

"I used to sleep in what will be your room this time around, with Marcus at the foot of the bed. He would wake me up with his whining and growling in the dead of night—I'd have to throw him outside just to get some rest. Marcus never seemed to like this place. He's more of a water dog than a guard dog. If there is an intruder, we'll probably have to fend for ourselves."

Jessica sighed a bit at the thought of keeping Marcus in her room at night if they were hit with a bout of rainfall and he couldn't be allowed to roam free. She scanned the somewhat overgrown front lawn leading to the dock for Marcus, before stepping inside through the house's side door that abutted the porch. The dog had not budged at all and had made no attempt to enter with them, persisting at his spot by the dock, his sight locked on the house.

April sat down next to Jessica at the kitchen table after they had finished filling the refrigerator from the cooler and stocking the pantry shelves from a few cardboard boxes that had been taped shut for the trip. Jessica had been talking at length while they stowed away their supplies and continued with the story that she had begun while unpacking. "So Richard and I went to Times Square for New Year's Eve. We saw a live show at Radio City Music Hall, and then we wanted to grab something to eat on the way back to the hotel. There was a Burger Mecca just a block from where we were staying, so we walked in and got in line to order dinner.

"Ahead of us was a customer arguing with the Burger Mecca employees who were behind the counter. He was waving his arms and shouting, demanding a refund for his meal but not getting anywhere with his request.

"With no warning at all—no one could have seen this coming, as the Burger Mecca workers hadn't even raised their voices to the customer during all this—two of the female crew members jumped over the counter and just started wailing on him. I mean, they were punching and kicking, and he was just taking it." Jessica hunched her shoulders and leaned in toward April from her chair, with a gleeful expression on her face.

"The man broke free from their assault, and they ran outside after him, pushed him to the ground, and there he was, getting his ass kicked in the snow." Jessica smirked while remembering the beating. "We decided to order room service instead."

"That's a terrible story. You have a mean streak, Jess."

Jessica smiled broadly. "I know. But you were always the good one, if not a little neurotic. A favorite of the holy sisters at St. Adjutor's. I never had the disposition for pious observation."

Jessica got up from her chair and said, "Time for me to hit the road. I'll join you next week after I go white water rafting with my brother and his friends. Then we can spend the rest of the month here relaxing before our internship starts. You can catch up on some reading during your alone time, like you wanted to."

April tried to seem pleasant. *"Anna Karenina* is tempting. I might be able to finish that in a week."

April watched out the side door window as Jessica drove off with Marcus in the back seat, leaving her by herself in an unfamiliar house. It was late afternoon, so April decided there was enough daylight remaining to take a boat ride around the lake and see the other side with the rental cabins.

The latter part of the day had become windy, and April let the strong breeze wash over her while standing at the edge of the dock. She noticed a metal rowboat on cinder blocks placed next to a nearby tree, its inverted hull pointing up. The rowboat had been painted aquamarine and looked spacious enough for two or three occupants. April was able to find the oars in the shed behind the house and then returned to the shore, pushing the rowboat out into the water and stepping into the boat as it drifted past the dock.

She rowed fastidiously and made good time across the center of the lake and then coasted along the tree line near the opposite shore to rest from her endeavor. The boat glided by the rental cottages—six unadorned units, all within several yards of each other.

April saw a stout middle-aged man moving among the cottages. He was wearing a canvas teal fishing hat and carrying tin buckets that he then placed at the shore near the red cedar wooden dock shared by the cabins.

The man had been watching April's boat askance as he laid down his burden. "Hello there, are you staying at the Snyder place across the way? The place has been empty since last summer."

April sat up in her bench seat and responded, "Yes, but we'll only be here for about a month. Do you know Jessica Snyder?"

The man shielded his eyes with a hand as he conversed with April. "Is that the daughter? I know that she stays with her parents each summer, but I've only talked to them, not her. Did know the previous owner, though."

April's boat came very close to the rental cabin dock and then halted its drift forward in the shallow water by the shore. The afternoon winds had died down and no longer disturbed the lake. The man continued speaking. "Name's Bill Patterson, miss. You are…?"

"April. Jessica and I are friends from school." April rested her hands across the boat's oar handles as the two spoke.

"The last owner was a big-time lawyer from somewhere out west," the man said. "Came up here for his vacations. I've been renting the same cabin here every year during perch season since there have been houses on the lake."

Mr. Patterson took off his fishing hat and put one hand on his waist, holding the hat above his knee with the other hand. "Watched them build that house on the other side, the one that belongs to the Snyders now." He gestured with the hat in his free hand in the direction of the solitary dwelling across the waters.

The orange glow of the day's last rays before sunset began to shimmer over the aquatic-plant-filled shoal between Mr. Patterson and April, signaling the need to end their conversation and row back to the lake house. But April had become curious about the owner before Jessica's family, so she continued. "Why did the first owner sell the house? Did he find somewhere else to take a break from his law practice or was it for some other reason? Just wondering."

"No, ma'am, Mr. Tinsley is passed away. He drowned in this very lake."

April was taken aback and now felt very uncomfortable returning to the unoccupied house by herself after hearing of the preceding owner's fate. Why hadn't Jessica mentioned this to her before she agreed to spend part of the summer at the house?

"I'm sorry to hear that. How did it happen? Wasn't anyone around to help him if he was swimming in the lake?"

"I warned Charles about taking a dip at night—he had a weak heart—but he may have done it on purpose too. No one knows for sure. Happened five years ago this summer." Mr. Patterson was noticeably upset but went on with his local anecdote.

"Don't know why he would have gone swimming at night, but the sheriff's deputies found his body on the lake floor, buried under layers of sediment. Lake Ultio is thick with freshwater plants, especially in the middle where it's deepest. They had to drag the bottom and haul him up with chains around his hands and feet. I saw the whole thing happen and what the corpse looked like after it was recovered.

"The Snyders had just bought the place from Mr. Tinsley, and he was getting ready to move out permanently the next day. They were staying at a hotel in town when it happened."

April looked away from Mr. Patterson and over the horizon, noting how little daylight was left. Even if the idea of being alone in a house with a checkered past didn't appeal to her, she didn't want to be out on the lake at night, either. "Jessica never mentioned any of this to me. She only said that her family has stayed at the house every summer, starting five years ago."

"They did. They moved in for a while after the death was declared an accident. Then they came back the next summer as if nothing had happened." Mr. Patterson replaced his fishing cap on his head and gave April a weary look.

"Good to meet you, Mr. Patterson, but I have to get back to the house. It's been a long day."

"Good to meet you too. I'll be out fishing all day tomorrow." Mr. Patterson extended his open right palm at April as a farewell and then stepped inside his unassuming abode for the evening.

April turned down the sheets on her bed and fluffed the pillows, flipping off the switch of the lamp on the nightstand as she lay at her side on the mattress. A dog-eared bookstore copy of *Anna Karenina* was close at hand next to the lamp, the evening's reading that had helped April unwind and ease her nerves after the day's disquieting revelation.

The dim radiance from the plastic night light plugged into a power outlet near the bed contrasted sharply with the total blackness that poured in from her bedroom window. A waning moon was barely visible over the peaks of the pine trees, and the kind of absolute lightless night only found in the deep countryside permeated the room, obscuring everything beyond the bedposts.

April drifted into a fitful sleep but after some time was able to find her first dream. She was out in the middle of the lake at night, sitting in the rowboat from her visit to Mr. Patterson. There was nothing discernible around her except the proximate murky lake waters and the perimeter of the boat, with all else being a yawning void. April looked down at her sandals and saw that brackish water had begun seeping into the boat from a hole in its floor. The boat was beginning to sink steadily.

While watching as the water filled the boat's interior, April stood and then dove into the lake head first in proper swim form. April hit the water with a splash and then attempted to paddle forward into the nothingness, but her partially submerged body was held in place by an unseen force. It was as if she was being pulled down into the lake by invisible attendants, grasping at her clothes and holding her legs tightly as she was dragged downward into the tangled mass of underwater flora. April struggled and attempted to tread water, but the lake was able to engulf her, her head abruptly disappearing beneath its surface.

She had inhaled and taken an emergency breath before she went under, but April's supply of oxygen was soon exhausted. She was hyperventilating and convulsing as her lungs filled with lake water, her nostrils burning from the unwanted intrusion.

April's vision grew dim as she ceased fighting, and she involuntarily choked up on the fouled water, but she was still able to make out a figure that was under the lake's waves with her, floating above her close to the surface...

April lurched forward in bed and gasped for air. She leaned onto her knees and consciously breathed until her breath had become somewhat even and normal again. Even so, she was inundated with a feeling of overwhelming sadness and loss that seemed to derive from nowhere. The nightmare had been so vivid; she had never dreamed of death by drowning before tonight.

A man stood at the foot of her bed and stared at April, bloated and saturated with lake water. He had clearly been underwater for some time, as he had aquatic plant debris in his dripping wet, matted hair, and his saucer-like eyes bulged horrifically. The man stood silently and said nothing, not making any motion at all but continued to gaze at April as she sat covered by her blanket.

Not sure if what she was seeing was more of the drowning nightmare, April crept out from under her blanket and onto the bedroom floor, reaching into the nightstand drawer for the crucifix that had been left by Jessica's mother. She knelt at the side of the bed and said the first Our Father, periodically glancing at the unmoving phantom.

> "Our Father, Who is in heaven,
> Holy is Your Name;
> Your kingdom come,
> Your will be done,
> on Earth as it is in Heaven.
> Give us this day our daily bread,
> and forgive us our sins,
> as we forgive those who sin against us;
> and lead us not into temptation,
> but deliver us from evil. Amen."

April continued praying a second Our Father followed by a third and then a fourth. The fourth Our Father provoked a reaction in the drowned man, as he took one step back from the foot of the bed and also become less defined, melding into the bedroom's outer darkness.

April watched him as she recited the next prayer, pressing the top of the crucifix to her chin. The specter retreated from her bed yet again as she prayed, and she could now see that the man's distended hands folded in front of him at his waist were chained together at the wrists.

April lowered her head and continued to pray, observing that each subsequent prayer would cause the apparition to step farther back and become increasingly faint. The Our Fathers continued until April could no longer see the dreadful figure in her bedroom. This was definitely no longer a nightmare, as April was sure that she was wide awake and could sense her heart thumping at breakneck speed as she uttered the words to the final prayer.

Barefoot and wearing only the soccer shorts and plain white T-shirt in which she had slept, she stumbled past the foot of the bed and dashed outside through the front door of the house. Breathing hard, April was about to flee down the path to the highway when she heard Jessica's voice call out for help. "Someone...I can't make it! I'm going under!"

She looked out over the lake shrouded in the nighttime sky and could see Jessica in the distance, flailing and attempting to keep her head above water. A slight man of about forty years old with horn-rimmed glasses suddenly ran up to April's side, oblivious to her presence, even though she was only a few feet away from him.

The man called out to Jessica, "What are you doing? Swim to the dock, and I will pull you to shore!"

"I can't. My leg is cramping, and I'm sinking. Get the sheriff... please!"

"We don't have time. I will swim out to you."

The man turned around and ran toward the shed. As he moved, April could see that he was almost translucent. He then passed April again, holding a flotation vest. The man removed his sweatshirt and waded into the dark waters of the lake.

He swam clumsily toward Jessica, the life vest strung around his neck, but she was far from the shore, and his progress was slow. The man paused his strokes to breathe and then asked while he treaded water, "Why are you out here?"

"I'm a star swimmer...thought I would be fine...but I can't move my leg. Hurry!"

The man resumed his efforts and reached Jessica, passing her the flotation vest. Jessica donned the vest and began to push herself through the water with her arms, back to land. The man did not move as she swam away but instead began to struggle to stay above the shallow waves washing over him.

He called out to her, "I'm having an attack. Jessica, come back for me! I can't make it without you." Jessica stopped and floated in place for a moment, facing the man.

Without a word, Jessica turned around and continued to swim back to the shore, overcome by her fear of drowning in the lake. As Jessica came within reach of the shoreline, the man's head went under the lake's waters once and then resurfaced, gasping for air, and then went under for a final time, sinking out of view entirely.

The vision ended as the early morning sun rose over the lake's tree line, bathing April in the light of dawn. She staggered back inside the house and collapsed on the living room couch, losing consciousness instantly.

"Did anything exciting happen while I was gone? Any of the local boys come looking for me, I hope?"

April met Jessica at the side door after watching her park her car near the shed as she had done before. Jessica was tanned from her outdoor excursion with her brother and seemed to be in high spirits.

"Jess, let's just go home. We can relax there—catch some movies, go shopping. It will be fun." April almost wanted to reveal her ordeal to Jessica but knew that she would be seen as delusional. Who could believe such a thing?

Jessica was adamant. "No, no way! We are staying put. I haven't had any quiet time since last summer, and I want to be rested for our internship. My parents and your parents are at home, remember?"

April smiled weakly. She vowed that she would never set foot in the lake house again after this summer.

"Where's Marcus?"

April looked behind Jessica for the rambunctious canine and then outside past the open door, but he was nowhere to be seen.

"I left him with my brother. We'll be fine. Marcus is sort of a pain, remember?"

"The house will be quiet without that dog. I'm going to get back to my novel if you have everything unpacked."

"Suit yourself. I'm going for a swim. Be back in a few."

Jessica walked past April with a carrying case and then minutes later came back out into the living room in a one-piece bathing suit. She was headed out of the front door for the sunny waters of the lake, a perfect day for a swim.

April looked around the corner into the hall that ran in front of the house's three bedrooms and the single bathroom. "Hey, why did you put your bag in my room? You can have a whole bed to yourself, you know."

Jessica stopped at the threshold of the front door and turned around to answer April. "I'm going to stay in your room instead, which is actually my room, anyway. I like the view of the lake better. You only have one bag, so just move it to one of the other bedrooms."

Jessica arched one eyebrow as she continued, "But what's with the crucifix above my bed? That's my mom's. Are you entering a convent? You just need a date, girlie, that's all."

April walked toward Jessica and furrowed her brow above her clunky glasses. "I feel safer with it over the bed. It's really a beautiful, hand-carved piece too. Leave it up, please, Jess."

"I was worried for a minute that you had swallowed all that hocus pocus. I'll leave it up…I promise."

Jessica stepped inside the front door several hours later with a towel wrapped around her waist.

"I'm going to change, and then we can play a board game. I know which one is your favorite," Jessica said, grinning. "The *Monopoly* box is in the linen closet, on the top shelf."

Jessica and April put the game box away after sundown and decided to go to sleep early. Jessica looked out of the large front picturesque window from the kitchen at the calm waters, which were barely touched by the faint moonlight.

"April, there is something I didn't tell you about this place…this house that we bought five years ago."

April was yawning but then became expectant, hoping to hear a confession from Jessica. "Yes? Is it important? I'm really tired and just want to get some sleep."

Jessica sighed and then gave her friend a genuine smile. "All right, I will tell you in the morning. Nighty, night. Don't let the bedbugs bite."

April moved her bag with her clothing and toiletries from Jessica's room and closed the door to the bedroom farthest down the hallway as she retired for the night. Jessica sat at the side edge of her bed with only the nightstand lamplight illuminating the open drawer in front of her. She stared at the crucifix she was holding in both hands, running a finger over its depiction of the Christ figure. Jessica put the crucifix in the back of the nightstand drawer and closed it, shutting off the lamplight. She decided that she would tell April about Charles Tinsley first thing the next morning.

April woke to a still house. She rolled over in bed and peeked at the clock on the nightstand. The digital display said 9:27 a.m. Jessica had not knocked on her bedroom door yet for breakfast, so April went into the kitchen and poured a bowl of cereal and milk.

"Jess? Come and get some breakfast. It will be lunch soon if you don't get up. Really. Jess?"

April went down the hallway from the kitchen and knocked on Jessica's bedroom door. No answer. She knocked again. "Jess? I'm coming in. I hope you are decent."

The shag carpet was drenched, and April's bare feet sank into the soaked fibers with her first steps into the bedroom. Jessica's body was sprawled over her mattress, the sightless eyes and slack mouth of her pallid, distorted face gaping up at the bedroom ceiling. Lake water ran in rivulets from her icy corpse over the bed sheets, dripping onto the floor around the bed that was littered with dead lake plants.

April gagged from the overpowering fetid smell of the drowned that permeated the room and wafted over her. She covered her mouth as she began to reflexively vomit, running from the bedroom tomb to escape its stench and the ghastly sight that lay on the bed before her. As she fled, April was able to glimpse that Jessica's right hand was clutching the nightstand crucifix.

GRANDFATHER'S CANE

"**I**s that Saint James or Saint John?" she thought. Megan continued to focus on the bare stone statue nearest to her, mounted on its pedestal along the church wall facing the side of her pew. The service had dragged on, and Megan felt herself beginning to nod off.

"They were both sons of Zebedee and Salome, but I could never tell one from the other—either from the statues or the paintings." A random thought came to her. "No, not *that* Salome."

The dim sunlight of the overcast day outside filtered through the stained-glass windows of the church, where the burial service was being held. Megan sat in the far back pew behind her family from which she could see Grandma Blindt's black pillbox hat and a hint of its mesh veil peaking above the burnished mahogany pew closest to the altar. The priest stood close to Grandma Blindt in the aisle between the rows of pews and had gone through the final recitation in the Book of Common Prayer, asking for a moment of silence to remember Grandpa Blindt.

The priest asked everyone to rise from their seats, and Megan was snapped out of her internal monologue, with her attention again on her grandfather's funeral proceedings. Megan straightened her skirt with her hands and stood with everyone else.

The priest concluded, "For as much as it has pleased our Heavenly Father in His wise providence to take unto Himself our beloved brother Walter Blindt, we, therefore, commit his body to the ground—earth to earth, ashes to ashes, dust to dust—looking for the blessed hope and the glorious appearing of the great God through our Savior Jesus Christ, who shall change the body of our humiliation and fashion it anew in the likeness of His own body of glory according to the working of His mighty power wherewith He is able even to subdue all things unto Himself."

The gathering of friends and family members then replied "Amen" as the priest put down his prayer book on the pulpit and signaled the elderly organist that the funeral service had ended. The breadth of the church's space was filled with the hymn being played, and the attendants began to file out into the center aisle from their seats to leave. Megan left her pew last and walked through the red ornate double doors of the church and down the shallow concrete steps, following her mother and father.

"Where is Grandma? Is she still inside?" Megan's mother, Claire, turned around and searched through the front doors, standing at the edge of the carefully manicured lawn surrounding the church. Claire was a broad-shouldered matronly woman, taking more after Grandpa Blindt than her mother. Megan was considerably shorter in height and really didn't resemble her family at all, either in her appearance or in her mannerisms.

"I'll go check. I don't see Grandma behind us, so she must still be with Grandpa's casket." Megan smirked at Claire and began to walk back into the church to find her grandmother.

The church itself was not particularly large but had a Gothic cathedral style that included statuary of angels and saints placed prominently among the arches of its interior. Four spires reached up into the cloudy afternoon sky that now showed signs of developing rain, one spire on either side of the façade of the church and the other two atop its gray shingled roof.

Megan saw Grandma Blindt seated in the front left pew, her eyes locked on her deceased husband's enclosed lacquered coffin. The casket was long and custom made, as Grandpa Walter had been a tall man in life, in contrast to Grandma Abigail's petite stature.

Megan walked to the pew and sat down next to Grandma. "I miss him so much. I can't stop thinking about him." Grandma took more tissue papers from her purse and dabbed her eyes with them. "I'm not sure how I can go on without your grandfather. He was truly my whole life after your mother and the other children grew up and moved away."

"Grandma, we all miss Grandpa Blindt, too. None of us expected this to be so sudden, but Grandpa is at peace now. A prolonged illness would have been much worse.

"C'mon, let's join the family outside. Uncle Harvey is going to take Grandpa's coffin to the cemetery now. The hearse is waiting."

Megan offered to help her grandmother up from her seat, but Grandma Abigail stood by herself and slowly made her way out of the church, putting the tissues back into her purse. The six pallbearers came for the casket and took possession of their burden, bringing it out of the open exit door past the rows of pews on the right side of the church.

St. Bartholomew's was at the intersection of a busy street in the town's downtown historical district. The church shared a few blocks with a small museum, a colonial-era boardinghouse, and the town hall. The town's main square was not far from the church and was a gathering place for the students of the sole local college.

Megan kept pace with her grandmother to the cars parked adjacent to the street curb, while a group of pedestrians gathered on the street corner opposite the church. Grandma Blindt stopped to speak to her daughter, who had been waiting for her mother to emerge from the church. Megan continued to walk toward the street, as her car was parked at the curb farthest from the church and closest to the street crossing.

Megan took the car keys out of her skirt pocket and glimpsed the busy street activity. She noticed an old man standing with his head down behind the walkers who were waiting for the signal light to change. He towered over the bunch, so he was visible even from behind them, but his posture was fatigued, and his shoulders slumped. The old man's wispy white hair was matted, forming a low crown around his otherwise bald head.

As the flashing light turned a solid green and the throng of people moved forward, the old man, who was dressed in dark formal attire, remained standing at the corner, with his face obscured. When the people reached the sidewalk alongside the church, the man's stooped neck shot up, and he gazed directly at Megan. His face showed nothing but complete, utter terror.

The man began gesturing and mouthing words that Megan couldn't decipher from her distance. His weathered face contorted itself, as if seized in some apoplectic fit. Megan then realized that the old man was Grandpa Blindt, watching his distorted, painful attempts to communicate something but with nothing produced that was perceptible.

A group of cars drove in front of Grandpa Blindt after the street light finished blinking amber, and he was gone after they passed. Megan stood silently in shock. "That couldn't have been real," she thought. "My grief must be much worse than I had imagined. All the stress must be causing me to hallucinate. I couldn't have seen that."

Megan pulled her thin-rimmed glasses off her face and rubbed her eyes, breathing slowly and deliberately. She stood still, tried to regain her composure, and then resumed walking as if in a mild daze. Megan settled into the driver's seat of her car and looked into the rearview mirror, now apprehensive that another vision might come to her.

She started the car engine and pulled out of the parking spot onto the side street that was parallel to the church. The funeral wake was being held at Uncle Harvey's house, which was an hour's drive from the church. Of all her adult children, Uncle Harvey lived the closest to Grandma Blindt, but his house was still considerably removed from the childhood home that their mother occupied to this day.

"Are you all right, Megan? You look like you've seen a ghost, if you don't mind me saying." Megan's father, Sean, met his daughter at the front door to Uncle Harvey's home and let her inside. The living room was full of the family's relatives holding drinking glasses and talking among themselves. Megan's mother was seated at the kitchen table in the adjoining room with a group of older women, deep in conversation.

Megan's father was younger than her mother, with a lithe build and a typically buoyant demeanor. The two had met during their college days and had started a family immediately afterward. Sean was a high school guidance counselor, and Claire was a science teacher at the same school. The three of them had travelled across the country to attend the funeral on very short notice, as Grandpa Blindt had not even been hospitalized before he passed away.

"I just need to sit down. Is there somewhere on the sofa I can rest?" Megan moved past Uncle Harvey and sat down next to some of her younger cousins with paper plates of food on their laps. "You'd better not spill any of that, Steve. Getting a beet stain out of this rug would be no picnic." Megan was attempting to change the subject and lose her father in the crowd.

"No, Megan, come and sit with us in the kitchen." Grandma Blindt moved toward her and stopped in front of her seated granddaughter. "I want you to tell Aunt Stacia and Aunt Betty about your plans for college this fall. You worked so hard for that scholarship, and I want to let the whole family know what you have accomplished. Grandpa would have been so proud of you."

Megan joined everyone in the kitchen and began explaining how she had won a full scholarship to study journalism at her mother's alma mater. "I am a legacy, so that may have helped as well. But Mom didn't study photojournalism, right, Mom?"

Claire looked around the guests at the table and said, "No, I was an organic chemist, but then I became pregnant with you followed by your brother. I've since been reduced to teaching an unending series of unruly freshmen the mole method. But you were worth it."

Aunt Stacia interrupted and said, "Claire was always so interested in Mother's farmers' almanacs and reference manuals on practical botany. All three sisters really loved reading, but your mother spent her four years at the Lyceum Academy with her nose buried in a book. We were quite surprised when your mother met Sean and got married. We didn't think she liked boys at all." Aunt Stacia winked and then smiled at Claire.

Claire grinned wryly and continued, "Megan is enrolled for her first semester classes but has yet to find a place to live. I insisted that she have no roommates during the first year of college to prevent any bad habits from forming, so the dormitories are out of the question."

Megan interjected, saying, "What kind of bad habits? You know, I could have matriculated at Carlyle House, which is all girls. Not exactly a den of iniquity, Mom."

Aunt Stacia turned her head away from Megan and looked at Claire, saying, "More like a nunnery. Claire, you should really let Megan have some fun. College is not only about studying and building a future, it's about—"

Grandma Blindt had been observing the conversation and then broke in, "The dormitories are very low rent, Megan. I wouldn't want you to spend any time in those. You can stay with me instead while you look for a suitable off-campus apartment. You'll be safe, I promise." Grandma Blindt now exuded a pleasant calmness, which was the first time Megan had seen her grandmother like this since the day before the funeral.

Claire became very bright and said, "Yes, that solves your problem, Megan. You can help sort Grandpa's things and clean up around the old townhouse. We will send everything that you have packed for school. Grandma needs someone right now, and we have to be back home soon."

Megan shifted uneasily in her chair but smiled compliantly at her mother. Megan had been to Grandma's house only a few times and never overnight. The two-story townhome on the corner of its residential street was filled with books accumulated from Grandma

Blindt's years of Latin and herbology studies. Megan could recall the musty smell from the leather-bound texts that permeated the second-floor pantry, overpowering everything else.

"Come up, I want to show you what's in the trunk." Grandma Blindt called down the short ladder leading up into the attic of the town-home. Megan had just finished moving her suitcase into the spare bedroom down the hallway from Grandma's room and had stepped out to face the collapsible wooden steps. "I'll be up in a minute. I need to see your bathroom first."

Megan headed toward the single lavatory but passed it instead. The upstairs kitchen and its pantry was the final room at the end of the hallway and held Grandma Blindt's small personal library. Megan opened the shuttered doors behind the kitchen table and observed the shelves of cookbooks and reference tomes. She stooped down to the lowest shelf and ran her finger over the titles of botany tracts about mistletoe, books on preparing animals such as sheep for supper, and an illustrated lunar calendar. Megan paused at a work that seemed particularly aged with a golden sickle on the spine. The sickle appeared to have been inked with real gold metal.

"Are you coming up or not? I want to show you a few keepsakes before dinner."

Megan rose up and replied, "Be there in a minute. I have to wash my hands and then I'll be done."

Megan started the climb up the steps, which required a firm grasp of the rails holding the steps together. The ladder to the attic was very flimsy and would have difficulty supporting any significant weight.

"Grandpa had to crouch down every time he came up here to put something away. He couldn't even use the ladder except to pull himself up into the attic. He didn't come up here that much, as it was a chore to do so."

Megan stuck her head through the opening in the attic floor and saw that it had a low ceiling with a semicircular Diocletian window, offering a view of the sidewalk outside the house. She finished her ascent and was able to stand upright next to Grandma Blindt, who was engrossed in digging through an open storage chest.

"Here it is. I haven't opened this scrapbook in such a long time. Your mother rarely came to visit, you know. We would always have to travel when we wanted to see them, which wasn't that often."

Grandma held a yellowed page from the journal in front of Megan for her to view. "Your grandfather and I were voted Homecoming King and Queen at the Lyceum Academy our senior year. This is us in the 'Chatterbox' section of the *Oakwood Observer.* Your grandfather was so handsome when we were teenagers."

Megan had never seen Grandma Blindt as a girl and was startled by how little she had changed over the years. Grandpa Blindt had truly exhibited his age and would have been almost unrecognizable from the confident, vital man standing next to the youthful Abigail holding the Homecoming prize in the newspaper picture.

"This same issue announced my second-place win in the Classics League national essay writing contest. My first year of Latin studies was entirely paid for by my prize money. I came right back to the Lyceum Academy after university and instructed classes in Latin. My firstborn—Harvey—put my teaching career on hold for a while and so did his siblings."

Megan took Grandma Blindt's hand away from the page and began to flip through the entries in the scrapbook. "Where is the article on the Classics League contest? What did you write about in Latin?"

"My mother never clipped it. She thought that studying the classics was a waste of time, but I was encouraged by Father. Most of my academic interests were due to his influence.

"I remember the write-up appearing several pages over from our Homecoming photo near the back of the same section. Perhaps you can put your investigative reporter cap on and find it for me." Grandma Blindt glanced over at Megan and raised her eyebrows slightly, with a hopeful expression.

Megan closed the scrapbook and passed it to Grandma Blindt. "Where would I find a decades-old local news story? Is the *Oakwood Observer* even being published anymore? I would imagine that it is not."

"Why, yes, it is, but at weekly intervals as it has been since the newspaper began printing. It shouldn't be too hard to find the archived copy at the library downtown, as there aren't that many editions to comb through. I haven't been there since I retired, but the whole newspaper catalogue should be tucked away in a backroom somewhere. I would be quite pleased to see it after all these years.

"Oh, and to answer your question, I wrote my essay on the Roman Legion. The Romans were victorious in battle because they were able to overcome their fear of death and fight as one, while their enemies couldn't summon the same fortitude or precision. *Vincit qui se vincit.*"

"Do you have any old photos of my mom? She was such a bookworm! I bet they are hilarious."

"Well, I have a few of her from high school. Claire was so awkward and shy that she didn't even feel comfortable being photographed. Her graduation yearbook is in one of these binders..."

"What's this?" Megan noticed an oak-wood cane with a silver metal handle in the shape of a ram's head with horns. The cane was leaning against the paneling along the wall behind the trap door to the floor below.

"Your grandfather had a slight limp the last few years. That cane belonged to my father, who brought it over from Wiltshire with us when we emigrated—right before my sophomore year of high school. After he passed away, I kept it as an heirloom of sorts."

The summer night's waxing gibbous moon provided a soft light in Megan's bedroom as she lay half asleep. Her mind was occupied with the events of the past few days and what was to come. Tomorrow morning would bring some apartment hunting and then a trip to the library to uncover Grandma's lost scholastic prize write-up.

"This bed isn't stable," Megan murmured. "A lumpy mattress and a rickety brass bedframe…" Megan rolled over and stood at the foot of the bed, stepping over to the open window with a view of the street. She paused and scanned the outside but saw nothing other than the next row of houses that continued after the intersection dividing the two blocks.

"Have to get some sleep. Don't want to use sleeping pills." Megan returned to bed with a loud squeak and began to drift off into slumber again.

The house was entirely still. Then somewhere down the hallway, Megan heard distant movement: the familiar creaking of the attic's wooden ladder buckling under a weight and the sound of something heavy being lowered onto the floor from above.

Then she heard one leaden footstep and then what sounded like a cane tapping the floor. Another step, and the cane again hitting the hallway floor of the silent house. One after the other and getting closer to the door to Megan's bedroom. Deliberate steps down the hall past Grandmother's room, past the bathroom, and then ending in front of Megan's bedroom door.

The loosely fitted doorknob to the bedroom rattled violently. Whoever was trying to enter the room was intent on getting in despite the lock. The vehement turning of the doorknob continued for a few more moments and then stopped abruptly.

A terror-stricken Megan continued to lie on her bed, fixated on the now quiescent bronze knob. Nothing further was heard from the other side of the bedroom door, and Megan fell into sleep without realizing it.

"I think someone was in the house last night." Megan took her chair at the kitchen table, while Grandma Blindt placed breakfast before her.

"Someone? You mean a burglar?" Grandma Blindt didn't take her seat and looked right at Megan.

"Yes. How could you sleep through all that noise?"

"I always sleep very soundly. I grow my own plants for special herbal teas. I have a nice cup of medicated tea before bedtime, and it relaxes me—I could sleep through anything. But what happened? Did you notice if anything was taken this morning?"

"Nothing seems missing, but I haven't been downstairs yet. I think there was someone outside my room. But it was very late, and I might have been dreaming. I would close the windows tonight just in case, even though we are on the second floor."

Grandma Blindt sat across from Megan with a worried demeanor. "I think it was just a dream, dear. But I will latch the windows this evening before we retire. We may get a chill, as the harvest season is approaching, so I will close the upstairs windows—irrespective of nighttime intruders."

Grandma Blindt produced a faint smile, and Megan munched on her buttered toast, pausing to speak. "You mean the fall equinox? I remember that from high school astronomy class. There is a fall equinox in September and a spring equinox in March. The equinoxes and the phases of the moon are part of the lunar calendar."

"You are correct, my girl. The harvest moon is the full moon that is closest to the autumnal equinox, and it is blood red in colour. *Et luna in sanguinem.*"

Megan wiped her lips with a napkin and left it on her plate. "I have to go and do some apartment hunting. I'll be back by dinner. Have to run, or I won't get anything done today."

"Will you find my news story? Swing by the library if you get a chance."

"Sure, Grandma Abigail. Be back soon."

Megan's curiosity had gotten the better of her, and she decided to take the bus to the library first instead of browsing through the listings for a studio apartment. Her scholastic course load wouldn't begin for a few weeks, and Megan assured herself that there was plenty of time to find somewhere to live. Exploring the library was too much of a temptation to resist.

A long set of stairs with metal handrails led up to the public library's edifice. The red-brown brick building was rectangular in shape and had a spacious reception desk at which a young woman was engaged in some paperwork. The worn maple wooden floors echoed Megan's footsteps as she entered the library and made her way to the librarian on duty.

"Hello, I would like to read some back issues of the *Oakwood Observer*. Are they in the stacks, or do I have to request them?"

The librarian put down her pencil and answered Megan. "They are on microfiche, if it is older issues that you need. What year are we talking about?"

"What is microfiche?"

The librarian continued to lean on the reception desk as she spoke. Her black hair was tied into a tight bun behind her head, projecting an overall appearance of neatness and efficiency. "I hadn't heard of microfiche either until I started working at the library. The microfiche machine barely gets touched as patrons don't research the *Oakwood Observer's* archives. Romance novels and magazines are generally what people borrow.

"The library stopped adding new editions to microfiche almost twenty years ago. The last two decades of editions are stored digitally on CDs that you can check out but not remove from the library."

"No, the news article I am looking for goes back many years. I require the entire back catalogue if I can get it."

"That shouldn't be a problem. If you've never seen microfiche before, it is stored in small plastic canisters. The images are compressed on something similar to a roll of film negatives. I'll show you. Please wait while I locate the box for the *Observer.*"

The librarian seated Megan on the chair in front of a battered Micron microfiche reader. The gray metal and plastic device occupied a single table among the book stacks at the back of the library. The librarian opened the first microfiche container and mounted the roll in the machine's spools.

"This is how you can view each edition," she said, turning the plastic control piece to move from each image to the next. "Some pages might be smudged or upside down, but use the knob below the frame to adjust the focus or rotate the image.

"Each canister in the box is labeled by year. These *Observer* newspapers are fragments from the town's history that are seldom discussed; you are a rare bird indeed.

But I will leave you to your work. Just let me know if you need anything else."

"Thanks, I'll do that."

Megan found the container dated with the year of the Homecoming article that Grandma Blindt had shown her in the attic and fed its roll through the spools. The viewing frame was lit up with black-and-white photos, and Megan zoomed through the front pages until she found the issue's Chatterbox section. At the back of the section was a small article with a write-up on the Classics League and Grandma Blindt's runner-up status.

Megan took a snapshot with the microfiche reader screen's copy feature and printed the page to the copier closest to the reception desk. The librarian saw Megan advancing on the copier and spoke to her. "Did you find anything exciting?"

Megan took the copied page from the tray and replied, "No, it's pretty mundane. A family member wanted something from the good old days. Nothing spectacular."

The librarian continued to speak to Megan. "There are some stories back far enough that makes one wonder about the town. I've read through the very old issues of the *Observer*, and you might be surprised at some of the things in there."

"Really? I have some time, so I guess I could do some further reading into the *Observer's* annals."

"Be my guest. We don't close for hours. You can soak up some of the town lore."

Megan returned to the microfiche reader and read past the end of the school-year issue into the subsequent months. The September issue had a story on a roof collapse at the Lyceum Academy, killing the Latin teacher and the assistant principal. The school blamed the tragedy on poor construction.

Megan began reading the next year's news, when she noticed the librarian standing behind her.

"Sorry to interrupt. It's just that you may be the only other person who has read these newspaper articles recently. The library is often almost empty, so sometimes I come back here and read the *Observer's* bygone issues.

"I see that you found the story about the Lyceum Academy. That is where the pattern begins."

"What pattern? A tragedy like that repeated itself?"

"More than repeated itself. There were two deaths, two disappearances, or a death and a disappearance in Oakwood every eight years after the Lyceum Academy classroom roof caved in, always in the month of September. It is the strangest thing I have ever seen. Let me show you something."

The librarian opened another microfiche canister and added it to the viewer's spools. She quickly turned the knob and arrived at a bold headline above a picture of two elderly women. "In September, there was a house fire that claimed two sisters who lived together. The police and the insurance company found that it was due to faulty wiring.

"After that there was a car crash that killed a young married couple, two young children vanished in the park at the edge of town, and there were several times in which two unrelated strangers went missing or died in September but otherwise had no connection to each other. I can show you the rest of the articles if you want to read more."

"No, that is fine, I believe you. But a few deaths every eight years aren't really a pattern; I would chalk that up to coincidence. People die all the time, even in accidents. But it would make a good horror story."

Megan presented Grandma Blindt with the photocopy of the *Oakwood Observer* page that evening, and Grandma put the paper into her scrapbook. All the windows were shut in the townhouse as Megan prepared for bed.

"I need some air. I'll open the window for a while and then get some rest," Megan thought. "I hope I don't pass out before I remember to close it."

Megan undid the latch and pushed the lower half of the window up and then locked the latch at the top. The full moon shone down on Megan as she paused to inhale from the nighttime atmosphere.

She crawled into bed and then heard the attic ladder lower itself outside her room. The house was quiet as it had been the previous evening, and Grandma Blindt had closed the door to her bedroom over an hour ago. Megan hoped that Grandma had somehow made it out of her room without a sound and was now coming back from the attic.

Heavy steps accompanied by the sound of a cane striking the hallway floor made themselves known to Megan. The mystery visitor from the night before had returned.

The cadence of footsteps and a walking cane continued and then ended at the threshold of her bedroom door. An unseen presence gripped the doorknob and shook it with great strength. Megan was sure that this was not a nightmare this time around.

As before, the doorknob was twisted from the outside for several more moments and then became noiseless as if it had never been disturbed.

Megan's first impulse was to throw open the door and confront her stalker; she was so seized with fear that she was no longer afraid and instead had become emboldened. Megan opened the lock to the door and stepped out into the hallway.

Grandma Blindt was facing her, holding a cup of tea in a saucer. "Let's go to the kitchen, my dear. I'll explain everything." Megan was wide eyed and breathing hard but followed her grandmother to the table.

"Here, drink this. You'll feel better."

Megan was speechless but did as she was told. The tea was warm and possessed a bitter but sweet taste, soothing Megan's throat as it went down.

"Did you see him? Where did he go?" Megan asked.

"Grandpa? He's around here somewhere; I'm not exactly sure where."

"Grandpa Blindt? Grandma Abigail, please, you're scaring me!" Megan sat down at the kitchen table and drank the rest of her tea.

"Your grandfather's spirit can remain on this plane as long as the second sacrifice hasn't been completed. Once the second death is accomplished, you will both be sent to oblivion. The Horned God will be satiated then."

Megan felt languid, and then a numbing sensation began to spread from her legs into the remainder of her body.

Grandma Blindt's relaxed tone changed, and her voice became malevolent. She leaned into Megan and said, "Grandpa wasn't trying to get into your room to harm you, Megan. He was trying to enter your room to warn you."

"You've poisoned me."

"Yes. I will dispose of your body and say that you left to start your classes. When you fail to show up, you will be listed as a missing person. *Non corpus delicti.* I'm so much older now that I can't get around the way I used to. I have had to find other ways to complete the cycle...with those closer to me."

Megan slowly slid down the kitchen chair onto the floor, feeling almost completely numb and unable to remain seated. As she began to lose all feeling and vision, Megan could sense a rope being placed around her neck by which she was dragged toward the bathroom. Grandma Blindt was surprisingly spry, with a powerful pulling vigor.

"When Julius Caesar and his armies first encountered the native Celts on what is now the British Isles, he wrote that these men believed that their gods delighted in the slaughter of prisoners and criminals. And when these captives were in short supply, they sacrificed even the innocent.

"I'm going to cut your throat in the bathtub, my dear. It will be quick."

RETURNED TO DUST

W arden Branko ran her index finger down a column of the ledger book's open page and then inscribed a figure at the bottom with her lacquer fountain pen. There were columns for a subject's name, inmate number, gender, age, place of origin, degree of health, assigned unit at the facility, testing series, and status (alive or deceased). Branko had tallied the number of subjects that remained viable upon completion of the previous day's testing regimen and had entered this number in the final row below the farthest right column of the subject journal.

Another shipment of prisoners was to arrive the next morning by train and be processed by Dr. Lutchenko's medical staff in preparation for a new battery of tests. Branko turned to a fresh page in the journal and noted at its header the date of the next delivery.

The light from the desk lamp dimmed as the orange glow from its bulb's dual filament faded out. The bulb cooled in its metal, halfspherical hood as Branko put the ledger in the top drawer, locking it with a small key. The windowless back office of the facility's main experimentation building was now unlit except for a shaft of light from the hallway guiding the camp's warden to the nearly closed door. The office's door bolt clicked behind her, and she strode down the corridor to the exit reserved for senior administrators.

The night sky above the campgrounds was starry and unobscured, owing to the remote, rural region in which the prison camp had been raised. The rectangular camp ran along train tracks that had been constructed a few hundred yards outside its barbed-wire fence's periphery, but there was otherwise no settlement or contact with the outside for, perhaps, a hundred miles in any direction.

The vast, towering mountain range at the foot of which the camp had been built loomed large in the backdrop as Branko walked past two armed guards and up the steps to her bunkhouse, retiring for the evening.

Lutchenko was hiding something about the only survivor of the latest round of psychotropic surgical probes, she thought. No one could withstand that kind of pressure in their brain and live...or Lutchenko had chosen to spare the girl from the full application for some reason yet unknown.

Branko had seen the film footage of Subject No. 4372 after she had been unstrapped from the procedure chair—the girl was shaken but she was fully conscious. The other subjects were lifeless in their seats, their eyeballs imploded after just one charged syringe injection through their pupils and into their retinas. The trial footage showed the girl staring into the camera as her cloth gag was removed by the examiner, her expression one of complete enmity and malice.

Camp Commander Volk was almost a head taller than even his tallest guard at the Science City Novbrok prison camp. He stood at the center of the processing platform, while the billowy smoke from the passing train wafted overhead. Dr. Lutchenko's assistant, Dr. Zhurova, waited next to him, holding an arch ring clipboard, her dull white lab coat flapping in the chill wind of the early day. The number of prisoners brought to the camp had become sparser with each new train arrival, as the fighting on the western front had worsened, and communication with the capital had become more infrequent. Shipments continued, however, with central command hoping that a major breakthrough from Dr. Lutchenko's research efforts was imminent.

Warden Branko approached the pair on the platform as the blue streamlined train came to a stop, and the attending guards opened the metallic boxcar adjacent to the back of the locomotive. A prominent red star was mounted above the locomotive's pilot, a symbol of the train's military function and affiliation.

"How many in this one? There are four sections of bunks to be filled after the rounds from the last two months. Dr. Podshivalov will receive a quarter of the new subjects at Unit 3 once they are processed. The remainder will go to Unit 5 for Dr. Lutchenko."

Dr. Zhurova stepped forward and extended her clipboard with one hand, showing Branko the list of persons being transported. "We require this entire group of new subjects. The attrition rate for Unit 5 is the highest among the units, and our work is the priority. Dr. Podshivalov must wait." Dr. Zhurova smirked, the corners around her full lips curling up. Zhurova enjoyed being insubordinate to Warden Branko and made full use of her status as Lutchenko's deputy investigator to exasperate the woman.

Branko looked into Zhurova's face and said nothing. The young doctor's almond-shaped eyes and straight black hair marked her as native to the camp's region, while all of the camp administrators and most of the guards were outsiders, from the west. Dr. Lutchenko had been the primary medical researcher at the Science City vicinal to the capital and was assigned to Novbrok for this reason. Lutchenko was only a civilian, but his influence was greater than either Warden Branko or Commander Volk with central command.

"I'll speak with Dr. Podshivalov, then." Branko's forehead tightened under the meticulously braided bun of blond hair behind her head in an attempt to hide her consternation. "He may not need another batch until next month."

Commander Volk had been ignoring the scene but now turned to look at both of them. "We may have to keep this group in quarantine for a week and observe them. What is being sent from the capital is deteriorating in quality, and these prisoners may be malnourished or diseased. Unhealthy subjects would be of no use to either Podshivalov or Lutchenko."

Volk's bearing and vitality cut a sharp contrast to the wretches stumbling out of the train compartment and being chained together by the guards. He showed no emotion from underneath his officer's hat visor as the train boxcar's passengers filed past the platform in a single line. The ragged cluster of men, women, and children were political prisoners and their family members, dissidents who were exiled to the Far East as a punishment for transgressions against the State and the people. No one expected them to return.

"The pineal gland is here, deep in the center of the human brain. The pineal is an organ that is only the size of a pea but may hold tremendous untapped power—power that could turn the tide of the war if properly harnessed." The chart of the sectioned brain was displayed on a full color sheet, hanging above Lutchenko's cluttered desk from a cord. The sheet was suspended from the retractable arm of the slide projector that had been placed squarely over a pile of the doctor's paperwork. Dr. Lutchenko continued to use his lecturer's pointer to emphasize his discussion with Warden Branko.

"But what success so far? I've read your weekly reports since these experiments commenced, and we have nothing but casualties. No subject has survived past the third trial, which is highly invasive, except for that girl you observed the previous week—Subject 4372."

Branko sat with one leg over the other in her high-backed chair in front of the doctor's desk, waiting for Lutchenko's response. The desirability of the germ warfare and hypothermia trials on the camp's subjects made practical sense to her and could save many citizens' lives. But this? Dissecting brains, digging around for some dormant biological relic from humanity's prehistory was akin to reading the entrails of a goat for portents. Only the strength of Lutchenko's reputation kept her from dismissing him entirely.

"Yes, Subject 4372. That is why I wanted to have this meeting with you, to convince you of our progress in the trials. She lived, whereas all the others have perished after the stimulant was applied. I would like to move to the fourth trial with her after further monitoring in isolation. We may possess in her that which I have been searching for this entire time."

"What does that wired syringe do to the subjects in the third trial? I must admit I don't understand all the technical details of your reports. I have watched films of each trial in my office. You have them bound in place in their seats and gagged. The subjects convulse after the injection but then slump in their seats. What is it that kills them?"

"An electroshock to their brains meant to stimulate the subjects' torpid pineal glands. The jolt is passed through the retina into the brain's cerebral cortex, which is the seat of our consciousness. The pineal gland is buried beneath the cerebral cortex, which is its gateway. Those born with the capacity to manipulate the pineal's psychic reserves will have their gland awakened and then be primed for the conditioning necessary to make use of its powers."

Branko leaned back in her chair slightly and looked Dr. Lutchenko over as he stood in front of his desk, grasping his pointer with both hands. He was quite an unassuming man with slightly stooped shoulders, bushy eyebrows behind round, tortoiseshell spectacles, and short, grubby fingers. But when the doctor spoke of a matter that was of importance to him, he became a giant both in presence and in manners. Branko could tell that Lutchenko truly believed that he was on the verge of uncovering something that had been a lifelong mystery to him, something secret that had been lost for untold generations.

Branko shifted in her seat again, adjusting the stiff woolen material of her uniform's skirt. This lecture was beginning to eat into her other duties, but she was willing to continue to listen. "Is all this just a theory? When did you begin to investigate the pineal and its supposed potential?"

"*Supposed?* I am a man of science, my little fox, and have demonstrable evidence to inform my theory." Branko would tolerate such language only from Dr. Lutchenko and no one else—and only in private as the two of them were now.

"When I was the principal investigator at Science City Obnesk, we used cadavers in our research but never live human subjects as we do at the camp. The necessities of wartime have changed everything. But there was one instance in which an exception was made for us.

"The police had brought us an old woman who was a local fortune teller. She had been accused of murdering her adult daughter. The corpse was littered with stab wounds from multiple kitchen knives; it was almost unbelievable that this frail, elderly woman could have held down her grown daughter who was in her physical prime and stabbed her over and over with every knife in their household kitchen. No one else was suspected, and the preponderance of the indicia seemed to affirm the old woman's guilt.

"The old woman was sent to the Science City labs because of something that had happened while she was at the metropolitan police station. The police chief had her committed to a solitary holding cell as they prepared the interrogation room for the woman's questioning. The woman was placed under watch with one officer outside the cell to keep her from possibly harming herself.

"Several of the officers were down the hall in the interrogation room when they heard a gurgling sound, followed by a thump as a body hit the floor. They ran out of the room to the woman's holding cell from which the sound had been heard, and the old woman's sentry was there gasping on the floor outside the cell, clutching his throat. This almost toothless old woman was standing still over the young man from behind her cell's bars, with a face that the officers described as 'being from Hell.'

"The officers threw open the cell door after unlocking it and shook the old woman violently until she released the young officer. He told the others what had happened, and they decided to bring the peasant woman to our lab. The police chief was a friend of one of our research scientists and knew that we conducted physiological studies at the Science City.

"We retained the old woman in a closed room with a bed, but she passed away in her sleep without warning during the third night of her stay at the labs. We had only been able to take some x-rays and blood tests before she expired. However, the autopsy revealed something very abnormal concerning the woman's brain."

Warden Branko had become quite intent as the doctor's story developed but now interrupted him to ask a question. "What about the old woman's remaining family? Didn't they want to claim the body of the deceased despite what she may have done to her daughter?"

"There was no other family. The woman and her daughter had recently moved from a tiny village near Lake Vodostok, where they had lived all their lives until relocating to the capital. The old woman was telling fortunes on the street up until the time of her arrest.

"But this is what we found after removing the old woman's brain. Even though her brain matter had atrophied significantly with age, her brain's pineal gland was massively swollen. And not only that, the pineal had grown from the base behind the cerebral cortex and seemed to actually have a path toward the frontal lobe—as if it could extend and then retract itself at will."

"So she was some kind of freak? Who knows what happens in those rustic areas near Lake Vodostok." Branko shrugged her shoulders a bit and then sat upright again.

"Not a freak," the doctor replied, "but more of a throwback to our precivilized ancestors...those who could use the force of their minds to execute their will on the physical world. The pineal gland was our species' third eye, a window into sources of now unimaginable cosmic energies that has since become dormant and enervated. But the vessel of this power remains, albeit in a degenerative state.

"Now think of what someone healthy and youthful with this kind of ability might be able to accomplish. If a feeble hag near death could hurl blades at someone and choke a grown man with but a thought, what might someone in the nascent stages of her pineal's development achieve?"

"Subject 4372."

"Yes, Subject 4372. I want to move to the fourth trial with her."

"And what constitutes the fourth trial?"

"A craniotomy. We will make an incision in the girl's skull, stimulate the pineal gland directly, and document the results. Her fully active pineal gland might then be trained as part of central command's Special Weapons Program. Our x-ray work after the third trial suggests that Subject 4372 may have a particularly enlarged pineal when considering the total size of her brain.

"Central command has research and evidence regarding these kind of subjects that they have, as of yet, held back from all of us, even myself. Our work here has encouraged them, as we may fill in the gaps in their own studies."

"Do as you would, Dr. Lutchenko. Let's just hope our diminutive patient survives this ordeal and becomes of use to the State."

Warden Branko left the sanguine doctor in his office and returned to her own to finish the day's administrative chores. Before taking her seat at a nearly empty desk (Branko was almost obsessively neat when juxtaposed against Dr. Lutchenko's Gestalt filing technique), Branko took a subject file from one of the cabinets along the office wall.

She sat at her desk and opened Subject 4372's crisp manila inmate folder. The girl's photograph was fastened with a paperclip in the folder's top right corner.

Alla Morozova was fourteen years old and was from a formerly autonomous region that had been absorbed by the State during the war. She and her parents had been at another camp, where her parents had expired. Alla had then been transferred to Science City Novbrok after "unusual behavior" was documented by the investigators following her parents' deaths. Alla had been assigned to Dr. Lutchenko's Unit 5 for this reason.

Branko put her hand over the photograph; the girl's atramentous eyes peered out at her. Alla was very typical of her home region's inhabitants, with wavy black hair and defined, aquiline features. But she had an almost timeless quality that kept Branko transfixed for an instant before closing the file and placing it inside her desk drawer.

The operating room's high ceiling lights were very harsh, and Dr. Lutchenko perspired lightly under his gray surgical cap. He looked out over the circular operating room and at the other members of the team. Dr. Zhurova faced him at the other end of the operating table, and two medical assistants were prepping various implements and surgical tools on a nearby cart. All four members of the medical team wore light-gray surgical scrubs and were protected from head to toe against exposure to the patient during the procedure.

The seats of the camp's hospital amphitheater were occupied by medical staff from the other research units, camp officers, and Warden Branko. Branko looked down at Lutchenko from her spot along one of the upper tiers of the amphitheater and watched as Subject 4372 was taken from a hospital gurney by two orderlies and placed on the operating table. Commander Volk sat close by, with two armed guards sporting submachine guns strapped to their backs on either side of the exit door.

Subject 4372's head was shaven, and she wore only a simple gray hospital gown. The girl was apparently unconscious as her neck brace was attached, as she did not move or show any other signs of awareness. The presurgery anesthetic must had already been administered shortly before the scheduled procedure.

Lutchenko and Zhurova had discussed using an awake brain surgery method on Subject 4372, but Lutchenko believed that the pineal would be the most receptive to stimulation while conscious brain functions in the cerebral cortex were passive. According to the executive briefing on the fourth trial, the same wired syringe with an electrical charge from the third trial would be injected into the area surrounding the pineal gland but this time through a hole made directly in the subject's skull. An exceedingly thin needle would be used to prod the slumbering pineal and provoke a reaction. The potential psychic response would then be measured by the electromagnetic field reader machines being wheeled into the operating room and positioned around the subject by more orderlies, which were followed by an electroencephalograph on a cart with its own monitor.

The machines hummed faintly in the background as Dr. Lutchenko addressed the amphitheater's assembled audience. "What you will witness today—I attest—is palpable evidence of an extrasensory reality beyond that which can be perceived with the five senses. Our subject is a germinating reservoir of an incredible, unrealized power that could change both the course of our conflict with the Alliance as well as the course of human history. Knowledge that may have been taken for granted by our remote antecedents will be brought back to the present and harnessed with modern science."

Dr. Lutchenko gestured behind himself with one hand while facing the observers sheltered behind the glass shields surrounding the operating room's enclosure. "These electromagnetic registers will record all field disturbances created by our subject once the pineal gland is stimulated. The subject withstood the application from the third trial, whereas no other subject from among over a dozen test groups had been able to do so. The stimulant used in this fourth trial will be of a greater intensity and also of a greater proximity to the gland. Let us now begin and move humanity out of the dark ages."

One of the assistants fitted Dr. Lutchenko's spectacles with a loupe that covered both lens and adjusted the device for comfort above his surgical mask. Subject 4372's face and lower scalp had been fitted with electrodes to measure her brain impulses during the surgery. The assistant handed him the first scalpel, and he proceeded to make a cut along the markings at the top of the subject's skull. Lutchenko constructed a skin and bone flap in the bare skull and then hovered the wired syringe over the opening that had been made. The extremely thin but stiff needle entered the opening that showed an exposed brain, and Lutchenko slowly pushed the plunger into the syringe's cylindrical tube.

Subject 4372's eyelids fluttered briefly, but then she became still once again. The electromagnetic field readers continued to hum, but their black-and-white cathode displays showed no new activity in the room's atmosphere. The nearby electroencephalograph read the subject's brain waves along its axes points, which were indicative of someone in a dreamless sleep state.

Warden Branko watched the operating room as Dr. Zhurova paced around the operating table taking notes, while Dr. Lutchenko looked down at the subject without a word.

"Durov, please continue to monitor the subject's breathing and pulse. There seems to be no reaction to the application at all. Something must be wrong."

Warden Branko pulled at her uniform's collar due to a growing discomfort. The temperature in the amphitheater was rising perceptibly even though the building itself had been cool in the early winter afternoon. She looked around and could see that the others among the rows were also feeling the room's climate change as they removed their hats and wiped their brows.

The wave on the electroencephalograph's monitor that had been steady showed a decline and then completely flatlined. "Dr. Lutchenko, the subject has stopped breathing. I can detect no pulse at all." Durov looked over at Dr. Lutchenko with a worried pause.

Lutchenko let out a deep sigh. "Zhurova, Durov, we are going to make an emergency attempt to revive her. If that fails, we need to at least recover as much of her brain as we can."

As Lutchenko turned away from the operating table, the air in the room crackled, and the electromagnetic field readers' displays surged with activity. The readers were now humming loudly, with waves cresting and falling rapidly in wild, oscillating patterns.

The glass shields partitioning the amphitheater seats from the medical team shattered abruptly and burst inward, showering the doctors with debris. Branko stood up from her seat and saw an ethereal form extend itself from Subject 4372's inert body on the operating table. The form began to take the shape of multiple stalks and washed over the stunned medical staff and the amphitheater's observers, into which they disappeared without a trace. A shimmering arm was approaching Branko as she hastened outside from the nearby exit and ran through the snowy campgrounds.

Branko turned around as lustrous golden appendages blanketed the campgrounds and engulfed terrified guards and the other camp personnel. Guards along the camp walls' walkways and sentry huts screamed and were then silenced as if they had been torn out of the fabric of space itself. An undulating mass of pure energy was forming a canopy over the camp but had yet to reach the front gates.

Branko continued to run, as the gates to the camp were now in sight. The snow-laden mountains past the railroad tracks might provide a refuge for her until the next train arrived. Branko turned again to see if there was anyone else making an escape as an iridescent blob that had begun to take the shape of an outreaching hand descended on her. Warden Branko cried out one last time.

"Everyone is gone. The camp has been abandoned." The battle-scarred commander stood behind one of the battalion's canvass-hooded trucks parked at the camp gates and spoke into his handheld transceiver. "Send a telegraph from the train station to central command, and let them know that Science City Novbrok is deserted."

Commander Mishin watched from outside the open gates as his men scoured the camp environs with leashed dogs, a light snow falling on them, hoping to find some sign of occupation. Mishin had been called in from the capital despite the approach of Alliance forces when no telegraph or radio transmittal had been received from Novbrok for several days.

"Commander Mishin, there is something in the hospital amphitheater. Please take a look at this." One of the field reconnaissance soldiers rushed toward Commander Mishin with an oddly excited expression on his face and stopped in front of him.

"What is this? Did you find someone alive?"

"No, but this is even stranger than all the piles of dust dotting the floors in the camp buildings. Lieutenant Toropov found it after we tried to use the radio set in the warden's bunk."

Mishin followed the battalion scout through the campgrounds and into the camp hospital. All the electrical equipment and light fixtures in the camp had been burned out, but it was still daylight, providing some measure of visibility within the vacant amphitheater.

"Here."

Among the shards of glass strewn over the operating room's floor was a table covered in gray surgical drapes but otherwise unoccupied.

"It's the burial shroud of a young girl. You can see the outline of her body over the length of the cloth. Her eyes, nose, ears, hair, all of it. The image is burned into the operating table's metal surface too."

Commander Mishin grabbed the cloth covering with both hands and held it up in front of him to view, thick dust falling off the cloth and onto the operating table and floor. A perfect replica of a girl's face gazed back at him, her eyes wide in amazement.

THE PLAGUE

"**R**ise and shine, Bartholomew."

Bart awoke while lying on his side. His freshly exfoliated face pointed at the wall paneling along the side of his bed as he felt the sting of adjusting his eyesight to a new morning after a night of sleep. Bart remained curled up under the cotton sheets, listening to his grandmother make her way around the room behind him. His nose wrinkled at a scent that he recognized but that was out of place indoors.

Bart felt some fingers touch his back. "Bartholomew, it is time to get up and do your chores. Don't be a lazybones. Your mother and sister need those bales brought down for the livestock." Granny's voice was unusually hoarse, almost as if she had been through a harsh bout of coughing.

Bart rolled over and gazed into his grandmother's face, which was now hovering close to his. Her features appeared blurry, and Bart squinted to focus on what was in front of him. He saw two gaping wounds where Granny's eyes should have been instead, set in her otherwise unmarred countenance.

Granny rasped, "Bartholomew, it's past daybreak, and your help is needed. I'll fix you some breakfast, and then it's off with you to your chores. Don't keep them waiting any longer."

Bart rolled over and bolted up, pushing himself against the wall behind his bed, the palms of his hands flat against its surface. He watched his grandmother motion her head back and forth as if searching for him; Granny seemed oblivious to her injury and just kept talking. "Bartholomew, where did you go? Are you getting yourself ready? I'll be downstairs in the kitchen making some eggs."

Granny stood from where she had knelt at the side of Bart's bedframe and began shuffling past the oaken study desk and stainless-steel coat rack, which were situated by the bedroom window. She was headed toward the bedroom door, her somewhat stooped form keeping its slow pace forward.

When Granny reached the threshold of the open doorway, she paused and looked to her side to speak, "Bartholomew, are you coming or not?" Granny remained motionless, with the profile of her head turned toward him as if waiting for Bart's response.

Bart was able to inspect Granny more closely as she stood in the doorway and saw that her floral apron was covered in bloody stains. Bart had noticed a pungent odor when he first became conscious, but now everything was fully registering following his sudden shock into wakefulness. He could also discern the handle of a butcher knife sticking out of Granny's left apron pocket with a deep red blot formed over the pocket's cloth.

Bart reflexively placed a hand over his mouth to muffle the involuntary scream he almost produced. His mind was racing, and he had trouble forming coherent thoughts. "Has Granny gone crazy? Where are Mom and Sis?" Bart lowered his hand and decided silently, "I have to make it outside. They can't be in the house unless Granny has already gotten to them."

His sneakers were under the base of the bed's headboard. Bart crept around the edge of the bedframe, reached down, and then put them on without tying the laces. He quietly stepped toward Granny and then inched his way to the narrow space between her and the outside hallway of the family home's upstairs floor. Bart could now see from his room that the cream-painted wooden rails leading up the stairs were smeared everywhere with blood.

"Bartholomew?" Granny stepped into the hallway past the bedroom's interior. Her back was now facing the room, and Bart slid past her and the bedroom door. He stopped his progress when he saw that Granny was reaching for the butcher knife in her apron pocket. Granny turned around so that she was facing the bedroom door with the knife drawn and said again, "Bartholomew?"

Bart leapt for the bathroom at the end of the hall, not risking the stairs. The bathroom door was slightly ajar, and Bart threw himself into the small space, surreptitiously locking the door behind him. He pressed himself against the door's white-coated paint, shut his eyes, and took long, deep breaths, before backing away to stand in the bathroom's center next to the sink.

Granny was walking around in the hall at what sounded like the top of the stairway; she didn't seem to be coming toward him. She called out to Bart, "I can't find my glasses, Bartholomew. Help me find my glasses."

Bart glanced down and saw two gouged eyeballs in the bathroom sink and a pair of bloody medical scissors on the counter. The shower curtain was in tatters and had been slashed in several places, while the bathroom floor was littered with tissue paper and other toiletries. Someone had been seized by an apoplectic fit in here and then torn into everything around them. Bart tied his sneaker's checkerboard laces and prepared himself for the climb down from the bathroom window.

He pushed up the lower half of the double hung window frame after undoing the latch at its middle. Bart stuck his head out the window and did a cursory survey of the grounds around his family's farmhouse.

He could see a thick pillar of pitch smoke reaching up into the otherwise clear summer sky from over the hills at Cassville, which was miles away from the family home. As the farmhouse had no immediate neighbors, Bart could observe nothing else and acted to fall from the second-story window.

He lowered himself by his hands from the window's opening until he was flush against the farmhouse's gray siding. Bart dangled briefly from the windowsill and then let go. He fell the short length to the ground and landed in the grass, making a quick recovery to stand on his feet. The smoke over the horizon had now become more prominent with multiple spires twisting in the wind, forming a tenebrous umbrella over the town.

Bart turned the old farmhouse's side corner from his bedroom window to its front and could then view the occupant of the broad porch that buffered the farmhouse's weathered doorway.

There was a figure seated in a rocking chair, rhythmically swaying with the balmy halcyon breeze. Bart's father sat in the chair with his head on his lap. The man's overalls were drenched in blood, and the head lay on its side with its eyes open, staring in Bart's direction but comprehending nothing. Bart summoned the strength to move forward and then kept walking, past the opposite front corner of the farmhouse to the barn, which was out in back.

Bart could hear the familiar sound of an axe hitting a log as his mother and sister entered his field of vision. Piles of timber were near the open double doors of the blue barn, but none of them was being struck. Bart's mother was, instead, removing his sister's left arm below the elbow with a chopping axe; the arm was partially cleaved but remained attached despite Mom's efforts. His teenage sister was standing over a tree stump bent at the waist, holding her arm out, while Mom laid another blow, this time severing the arm completely.

The mangled arm fell off the stump into the gore-splattered dirt surrounding it. Bart's sister staggered a bit, corrected herself to stand upright, and then beamed from ear to ear. Both women giggled obscenely, while Mom handed Sis the axe, before kneeling down at the stump and extending her own left arm over its surface. Their faces were markedly streaked with cruor, in the pattern of dried tears.

Mom glimpsed Bart when she turned her head and abruptly snapped up from her spot at the stump. Both women let out a bizarre keening in unison, their expressions glazed with madness, red-rimmed eyes blazing with an almost religious fanaticism.

Mom grabbed the axe from Sis and dashed at Bart with the weapon raised over her head. Sis followed, waving her amputated limb before her, a thin stream of blood blotting the mowed grass beneath her feet as she ran.

Bart lurched and sprinted in the direction of the highway, which passed the boundary of the farm's crop fields. He didn't dare look behind as he ran—his family members seemed to possess almost preternatural speed. Bart ran faster than he had ever run in his life, even as the thumping tracks behind him faded into the distance.

The highway was empty once Bart reached its paved lanes, and he continued to run. He passed a car that had been abandoned in a ditch, its emergency lights blinking from the tail end that faced the highway from its resting place. Boxes were tied to a rack on the car roof, the supplies of whoever had tried to leave Cassville but had failed.

Bart started to come to a halt only after his lungs began to burn from their exertion. He stumbled and sat himself in the gravel on the side of the highway, regaining his breath after a while, and then sobbing at his loss. Mom and Sis were long gone behind him.

Bart continued to sit at the periphery of the highway, his arms resting over his crossed knees, his brain reeling from all that had transpired. "My God, what is going on? They were mutilating themselves. The same thing must be happening in Cassville." He looked over the pastureland from his vantage point on the road and could see no one else.

As Bart dusted himself off to continue, pressure began building in his right ear, causing him to rub it in hopes of clearing the sensation. The pressure spread to his left ear, and a subdued, sinusoidal humming then became noticeable. The pulsating hum started to overwhelm the ambient noise of the outside and fill Bart's skull with a mounting, nearly unbearable tension.

"Ahhhh…" Bart tried to speak, but no words came forth. The pulsating hum clouded his sight, with the hills, the fields, and the highway being replaced by a brilliant white light.

Bart fell over, hitting the tarred curb, clasping both his ears with his hands. The humming became a dull but all-consuming buzz, so loud as to preclude cerebration. Bart clenched his teeth in agony and continued to shield his ears, in a vain effort to block out the roaring ocean of sound.

Then it stopped. His back was bruised from where he had fallen on the curb, but he was able to sit up in a daze. Bart could feel something moist on his skin, so he touched his cheek. A small amount of blood had flowed from his right eye socket and formed a rivulet across his face, which was now dripping onto his T-shirt.

The sun was at its golden hour when Bart passed the "Welcome to Cassville—One Great City" sign after the highway exit. The dimming sun's radiance from behind the stylized, antiquated sign was adequate enough to view the buildings below the off ramp from the highway, which showed evidence of extensive looting and vandalism. Bart could see no movement from either cars or townspeople as he descended the highway's off ramp to the town's main street.

The exit to town was blocked by a pile up of burned-out cars that were smoldering and exuded a gasoline smell, around which were strewn glass shards and the contents of luggage from fleeing passengers. Bart did not want to peer into the car seats as he walked by, for fear of what he might witness.

"Everyone is gone. Not a soul alive in Cassville," Bart whispered to himself. The bright pink exterior walls of the Hen's Roost Diner were blacked by fire, with every one of its windows broken in. As with the highway scene, the cars in the parking lot had been torched, doors welded together by the intensity of the heat.

Bart stood on the steps of the Hen's Roost, which were strewn with debris from whatever carnage had taken place there. The patron booths and the countertop were no longer fully visible, as they had been partially buried in emptied boxes and broken items from the kitchen. Bart stepped inside through the open door and could smell that the diner's grill had recently been used to cook some kind of meat in apparently large quantities.

The double doors to the back kitchen area were open and had been splattered with gore that was now drying but still gave off a strong odor mixed in with the cooked meat and burning diesel smell. Bart pushed his way into the back kitchen and then saw all of them.

Bodies were stacked up in several piles, reaching to the kitchen ceiling. There must have been fifty people in those piles. Limbs had been hacked off, and many of the bodies had been eviscerated. Those corpses that were still whole had been contorted into abnormal, almost impossible shapes, feeding the grotesque nature of the scene.

Bart felt a strong sense of fear upon seeing what had happened and could now guess where the grilled flesh from the diner had been obtained. The floor was sticky and wet with blood draining into the grates between the commercial sinks that had been used as an abattoir. Bart opened the door of the walk-in freezer connected to the kitchen and saw that several more bodies had been hung on hooks, with plastic bags of body parts and internal organs stacked on metal wire shelves along the walls of the freezer.

Bart ran out of the diner and into the deserted street extending through the center of town. He passed more burnt-out cars, ransacked homes, and looted businesses until he reached the parking lot of the small county hospital that was near the next exit to the highway. An ambulance had been overturned and set on fire, and the cars in the parking lot were also burned out. Evening had come upon Cassville, and the only light was from the artificial glow showing from inside the hospital lobby as Bart made his approach.

A number of the florescent tubes used in the ceiling fixtures hadn't been smashed and provided some visibility within the devastated lobby. Bodies of hospital staff and patients had been piled on gurneys and pushed into the open rooms adjoining the lobby area. A faint hissing emanated through the hospital's intercom with the noise of something moving around in the distance being picked up by the system's open mic.

Bart didn't want to risk staying inside the hospital. He thought, "I need to find a vehicle somewhere to drive away and make it to the city. The delivery trucks out in back might still be in one piece. It's worth a shot."

Bart strode out into the dark and onto the lush, well-maintained lawn surrounding the hospital building. A chorus of summertime crickets could be heard, but the environs around the hospital otherwise seemed devoid of life. Several more bodies of patients or staff that had been hurled from the hospital upper levels' many broken windows dotted his path to the loading area in the back of the building.

A body that had been crushed by the force of its impact was dressed in cerulean colored medical scrubs and was lying face down. An ID badge was a few feet from the body's resting place and read, "Douglas Vuković, Resident Practitioner." Bart continued to walk, weaving around the deceased, and then saw the corrugated iron platform of the hospital's loading area.

The loading area's garage door was locked and must have remained so during the chaos at the hospital. An empty truck trailer without a diesel cab was positioned on stilts, blocking the employee parking spaces that were allotted to this area. Bart turned the corner of the truck trailer and saw that one standard-sized delivery truck was parked by itself.

Bart hurried to the driver's side door and saw that it was unlocked. He quickly opened the truck's door and jumped into the driver's seat, closing the door behind him. The truck's cab was unlit, but Bart was able to find a small flashlight in the glove compartment.

Bart had hotwired trucks on the farm, so he hoped that he would be able to do the same with the delivery truck. The glove compartment was still open, so Bart shone the flashlight into its space. A utility knife was in a plastic pouch, and he grabbed it to use as a tool.

The plastic cover on the steering column was wedged tightly in place, but Bart was able to pry it loose with the knife after removing the screws. A bundle of wires fell from the access panel into the barely visible space below the steering wheel.

Bart placed the flashlight handle between his teeth and aimed its light into the panel with the hanging, colored wires. He traced the wires with the color that he concluded indicated ignition and battery, from the experience he had working on older trucks, and found they led straight up into the steering column. Bart stripped the insulation from two of the wires and twisted them together.

The interior lights came on with a jolt, and Bart dropped the flashlight from his mouth into his hand. He found the starter wire and stripped some of the insulation off its end. Bart touched the live end to the battery wires, and the truck engine revved slightly. He put pressure on the gas pedal, and this time the truck revved loudly, settling into a steady rhythm as the engine continued to pump.

There were no lights visible from the truck's cab with minimal illumination from a clouded moon. Bart could see nothing around him, so he turned on the truck's headlights. The headlights flashed on and lit up the concrete divider between the parking space and the line of trees planted in a row near the hospital's outer lawn. Bart heard a keening sound somewhere off in the distance.

The steering column was locked, so Bart searched for the keyhole near the wheel and popped the spring with his knife, breaking the lock. The keening sound was growing louder and was originating from the direction behind the truck.

Bart put the truck into reverse and immediately slammed into something weighty that was not visible from the rearview mirror. He put the truck into drive and spun it around, now facing the loading area of the hospital from where he had found the parking spaces.

There was a crowd of several dozen people running rapidly toward him over the hospital grounds. The keening sound had become saturated and was drowning out the sound of the truck motor as the crowd reached the loading area.

As Bart drove forward to reach the roadway in front of the hospital, a figure sprang from the darkness outside the driver's side window and attempted to pull open the door of the moving vehicle. It was a young woman, whose long hair was partially ripped from its roots, her face streamed with blood; she was snarling and yanking at the door to Bart's compartment. The girl's teeth had been filed into sharp points with an implement.

The girl let out the unnatural, ear-splitting keening that Bart had first heard at the farm and ran alongside the truck as Bart made his escape. She hung onto the driver's side door and took out a large knife with her free hand.

Bart accelerated and attempted to lose her as he barely missed the throng of enraged townspeople wielding axes and bats. Bart heard bodies hit the back of the truck, and the young woman fell off, rolling onto the lawn along the hospital's walkway. The truck was now speeding over the main road through Cassville and then onto the highway leading out of town, its large back compartment shifting and rattling as Bart drove up the exit ramp away from his attackers and into the desolate night.

The four-lane highway was flanked by rows of deciduous trees in full summer bloom on either side as Bart drove through the countryside. The night was almost entirely dark with negligible moonlight and a dearth of cars on the road. The chugging of the engine and the wheels turning over asphalt were the only sounds Bart could perceive as the truck's headlights pierced the almost impenetrable blackness before him.

Bart thought about reaching the city, but he considered that it would also be overrun, not knowing how far the insanity had spread. What could have caused this to happen? Has everyone become possessed? "Why haven't I been overtaken by whatever is causing this plague? That buzzing I heard earlier..." Bart hoped to find other survivors, but so far everyone had either become a killer or a victim, besides himself.

Bart flipped on the truck radio and cruised through the AM dials. There was a good deal of static, but Bart was able to find a local news station. The announcer was reading from a statement.

"They are advising everyone to remain in their homes and not to attempt to leave. The Air National Guard will announce when evacuees can be transported to a secure facility. In the meantime, please remain in your homes."

The truck drove slowly up a steep hill and then reached its top. As it made the descent down the hill, the beams of another vehicle's headlights came into view. Bart braced himself and hoped that this was a sign that the city or another nearby town had escaped whatever had infested Cassville and his family's farm.

"No urban center is safe at this time. If you are presently outdoors in an urban center, you are advised to move to another location and seek fortified shelter immediately."

The vehicle's high beams became more intense as they approached Bart's truck, which was moving at a constant pace. The vehicle's occupants were driving at a tremendous rate and passed Bart's truck on the opposite side of the highway almost as if it were standing still. Bart could hear its wheels screech to a halt far behind him and then the sound of the vehicle barreling forward again.

"There are widespread reports of cannibal..." Bart turned the radio knob off and gripped his steering wheel for what appeared would be a fast-moving assault.

Bart could now see from his side-view mirror that the vehicle was a pickup truck. As the pickup truck approached, its high beams shone brightly, making it difficult to see any passengers. Bart tried to accelerate his aging white delivery vehicle with its heavy payload, but he was effectively a slow-moving target on the highway as the truck decelerated and pulled along the driver's side flank.

The reflection of both vehicles' headlights revealed that the truck was festooned with dismembered human limbs and heads strung over its front hood with rope, and graffiti spray painted over the entirety of its outer body. Bart couldn't see the drivers in the truck's cab from his higher position, but the truck's cargo bed held a half dozen crazed occupants armed with axes and baseball bats.

As their truck kept pace with Bart's vehicle, one of the men seated in the cargo bed climbed to the top of the truck's cab roof and supported himself as the two trucks continued down the highway. He stared menacingly at Bart from his perch and put a large hunting knife between his teeth to free his hands. Bart could see that the man's face had been heavily scarred with sharp objects, almost in a ritual fashion, as well as exhibiting the telltale bloodstained tear streaks he had noted on the girl at the hospital and on his family.

The man was poised to leap, when Bart suddenly hit the delivery truck's breaks and receded behind the still-moving pickup truck. The armed man fell into empty space and bounced off the highway's pavement, flopping into a ditch by the roadside.

The pickup truck was not moving as swiftly as it was when it first approached, so the drivers easily swung their vehicle around and came directly at Bart's truck, which was now stationary on the highway. The length of the delivery truck was perpendicular to the four-lane divide, and its back compartment was exposed to the on-coming transport and its crew.

The pickup truck careened into the side of the delivery truck and spun it off the highway from the tremendous force of its impact. Bart was buckled into his seat but his chest slammed into the steering wheel as his truck spun again and again until it hit the tree line off the highway. He was only partially conscious when he heard a deafening explosion and saw the glare of flames in his driver's side mirror.

The shattered windshield let in the morning sun, and Bart carefully sat up in the driver's seat. Bart felt his face and chest, examining himself for any obvious signs of trauma. His thick curly black hair held flecks of glass from the accident, which he brushed out with a hand while closing his eyes. The cab's rearview mirror showed no cuts or bruises on him, and he could feel his legs, so Bart unbuckled his seat belt and opened the delivery truck's driver-side door.

The air was acrid with burning gasoline, twisted metal, and blasted corpses. Bart stood beside the delivery truck, facing the highway from last night. The now blackened pickup truck rested in the middle of the highway, still smoldering. The desiccated assailants lay strewn around the finished hull of their means of attack, victims of the broken fuel line that resulted from their collision.

Bart walked around to the other side of the delivery truck and saw that the back compartment had an enormous crater in its center. One of the truck's back wheels was missing, and his means of transportation was otherwise out of commission. Bart lowered his head, rubbing his stiff neck, and contemplated his next action.

"Put your hands in the air where I can see them. Right now!" Bart heard a woman's voice behind him. He gulped and put his hands up over his head, showing that he was weaponless.

"Now turn around, be slow, and let us see your face." Bart did an about face and saw two young women, one holding a single barrel shotgun that was pointed at his head from several yards away.

The unarmed woman spoke up. "He doesn't have the marks. He looks clean."

The woman leveling the shotgun at Bart interjected, "What's your name? Say something!"

"Bartholomew." Bart let his parched mouth hang open. He saw that the women were dressed in blue jeans and T-shirts and did not seem deranged as all the others had been. The fact that they had not attacked him instantly was more proof in Bart's mind that they were sane and might help him to survive.

"Lisa, search this boy for weapons." Both women were in their twenties, but Lisa was probably the younger one. She walked forward, scrutinized Bart's features, and began searching his shorts pockets. Other than sneakers, Bart was only wearing athletic shorts and a thin T-shirt, so there weren't many places to hide a knife or a gun. The girl ran her hands over his chest and back and then stepped backward, still watching Bart.

"He's got nothing. Looks like you slept in those clothes. Where are you coming from?"

"Outside Cassville. The whole town has been destroyed. Is this everywhere? Can you tell me about the madmen?" Bart kept his hands up and hoped there was a way out.

"It's everywhere. The radio says that all the cities have been overrun. We can't get a TV station anymore. You can put down your arms now."

Bart lowered his arms and put them slack at his sides.

"This is Lisa, as you heard, and I'm Emily. We're sisters, and we're all that's left of our family. We need to get off the road and to the house before someone sees us."

Emily then got behind Bart with her shotgun in both hands and motioned for him to move forward, gesturing with the barrel. Bart followed Lisa, and the three of them stepped off the highway and into a forested area that extended into the hills.

"We heard the explosion last night and thought we should come down here in the morning just in case. You must be the only survivor then."

"Those men in the pickup were insane. They collided with me, and I was pushed off the highway." Bart turned back to look at Emily and motioned with his right hand. "They rammed my truck, but it ended up killing them."

"Yep, they were insane all right. Almost everyone is now. You are the first we've seen who hasn't turned."

They continued along what was now a dirt path running through the woods. A two-story Victorian-style house was up the hill where the trail ended.

"We're up here. We're connected to the highway by a road that only runs past us and then finishes at a dead end. We have to keep the lights off at night so we aren't visible from the highway."

Bart stepped into the thicket and pulled himself up by the young branch of one of the downward-sloping trees. It was a short climb over the hill and into the fenced backyard of the house. Lisa opened the gate and let them into the enclosed yard.

"We lock this up at night too. We've boarded up the windows on both floors from the inside. It's not a fortress, so we might have to barricade ourselves in the basement if things get rough enough."

Bart observed that the yard had a freshly dug mound about ten feet long near its shed. As the two girls and Bart walked onto the house's back porch and opened the door leading inside, Bart could see that chunks of the porch's wooden columns had been blown away with a firearm.

Thin rays of sunlight penetrated the gaps between the boards covering the picture window to the living room. Emily sat down on an upholstered sofa and put the shotgun across her denim-swaddled legs. Bart stood and accepted a glass of water from Lisa, which he guzzled down.

"I could use another one...or two. Where is the kitchen?"

Lisa led Bart to the kitchen lined with cardboard boxes along its single wall, and he drank deeply from the faucet. "I don't have to remember my manners if this is the end of the world." Bart tried to smile at Lisa, but she just watched him wipe his mouth.

Emily turned on the handheld radio that was sitting on the end table next to her sofa. The sound was somewhat muted, but Bart could hear it from the kitchen.

"The military has begun burning bodies in mass graves. The Center for Disease Control doesn't know why this is happening or where its source might originate. They are taking no chances, as..."

Emily turned the radio volume down as Bart and Lisa sat across from her on another living room sofa. "What happened to your family? Did they all turn?"

"Yes, my mother and sister tried to murder me right after my grandma tried to do the same. I ran to Cassville and saw what had become of the people there. A mob almost surrounded me, and I drove away when I got into the fight on the road."

Lisa turned to Bart and leaned in. "Have you heard the buzzing yet?" Lisa's face gave away no emotion but Bart could tell that she was clearly agitated when asking the question.

Bart was startled and looked at both of them, saying, "You've heard it too? I felt like I was splitting in half, and then it just ended."

Lisa got up from her resting place on their sofa and walked over to sit next to Emily. They both stared at Bart and were silent for a few moments.

"We were eating breakfast when the buzzing started. Emily and I were in the kitchen and collapsed from the pain. The buzzing seems to be out of this world—it's no earthly sound at all."

"Like you, the buzzing ended for us, and we could stand again. I went to the back door to find our parents and stood right there." Emily pointed at the braided throw rug in the entranceway. "I looked through the side window, and saw our mom and dad eating our younger brother in that yard. They had cut his head off with a shovel and were tearing at his bare arms with their teeth."

Lisa stood up and turned away so Bart couldn't see her expression. Emily continued. "I ran upstairs and grabbed our dad's pump shotgun out of the bedroom closet where he kept it. They were finishing the legs when I threw open the door and started firing. I was able to bring both of them down without reloading. I hit the porch a few times. All three are buried out back."

"Why do you think we didn't go mad? The buzzing must be what changes everyone. I bled from my right eye after the buzzing, and all the crazies have blood marks all over their faces—their own blood."

"We don't know. The buzzing is like a wave washing over a shore and then receding. Once someone is trapped, and they aren't swallowed up, it passes over them. The radio has mentioned the buzzing, but there are some who haven't heard it yet."

Bart, Lisa, and Emily remained huddled around the tiny radio and listened as the signal faded in and out. Reports came in over the course of the day that indicated the military was losing ground and had to fall back, as so many bases and camps had been compromised. The radio-station announcer at one point mentioned that he had barricaded himself inside the station building.

"The streets outside are filling with throngs of butchers, parading their ghastly trophies. I am not sure how long I can continue this broadcast. An armed guard was planning to arrive to escort us to safety—if anywhere is truly safe—but they never appeared. It is only a matter of time before those below make it up to the fifth floor..."

The evening turned into another moonless night. The battery-powered radio crackled, and Emily hunted through the dial for a viable signal, but some had gone out completely. The sound of a diesel truck driving and then coming to a stop nearby issued from the road outside the sisters' house.

Lisa ran to the front door and looked through the small window in the door frame's apex. Lisa whispered over her shoulder, "It's a trucker with no load on the road outside in front of the house. He's only driving his cab."

The three of them had been sitting in the living room with the lights off, as electricity had stopped working before sunset. Emily had lit some candles that were placed on the floor, away from the windows, but she turned on her flashlight and approached the front door. The diesel truck was parked directly in front of the house with its engine off, but its headlights shone into the woodland blackness surrounding the home's front lawn. The crew cab was silver colored and bore the company name "Ward Trucking" detailed into its driver's side door, which was visible from their hiding spot.

"Lisa, that's Uncle Phil's rig! He is alive, then! We have to go outside and get him in here."

Lisa put her hands over the front doorknob and said, "Wait. How do we know that is Uncle Phil? Some of the crazies might have just gotten his truck and drove it out here. Let's see if he steps out and shows himself first."

Nothing stirred from within the cab while the truck's high beams shone into the ring of sparse trees at the country road's dead end. Lisa and Emily were too far away to determine if someone was even in the cab at all.

"We have to check. I'm bringing the shotgun. Hold the flashlight for me." Lisa took Emily's flashlight as Emily returned to the living room to fetch the pump-action shotgun. Bart followed Emily to the front door, and they walked outside together to stand on the lawn a few yards away from the cab's sealed and darkened enclosure.

"Phil, is that you? We need to make sure that you're OK." Emily held the shotgun in both hands but pointed its barrel away from the cab. "Phil, open the door if you're all right."

The door to the truck's cab flung open, and a misshapen man thing spilled out, charging at Emily. Part of its once-human face was deformed so that the right eye had become gigantic and bulbous, and its gaping mouth was filled with sharp, horn-shaped teeth.

The creature let out a hideous croak as it battered an aghast Emily with an elongated, suckered tentacle where its right arm should have been instead. Lisa shrieked and watched Emily drop her shotgun on the ground as she was choked to death by the tendril wrapped around her throat. Bart turned toward the house's front porch to flee but was pulled off his feet by a second tentacle emanating from the monstrosity's torso.

On the living room table, the radio's news broadcast signal ebbed and was gradually replaced by a sinusoidal humming from within an inhuman voice uttered a mantra over and over: "The Great Egg has opened...it has awakened. The Great Egg has opened...it has awakened. The Great Egg has opened...it has awakened."

ROADSIDE DINER

The In and Out Diner was on an infrequently travelled high-way off the main interstate. Traffic was heavy in the diner's early days, but continued construction on the main inter-state diverted more and more customers away from the diner and to other pit stops along their journeys. Drought, local people moving away, and falling tourism meant that the diner was almost empty on most nights, save for some die-hard loyalists and scattered truckers passing in the dead of night.

The night Patrick McKinney visited the In and Out Diner was one such night, having become lost during a cross-country trip to his brother's family home for the holidays. Patrick was alone in his four-door sedan as he glided into a parking space in front of one of the diner's windows. He had seen the florescent sign "In and Out Diner" with a few faded letters from the empty two-lane highway and did a quick turn for some coffee and directions.

What I am going to relate to you may seem unbelievable, but it truly is what happened. I am not superstitious, nor have I ever held any thoughts about the supernatural until that night. My only hope is to warn others about "Them" before it may be too late. "They" are every-where, even though hardly anyone even realizes it. "They" are only seen when "They" want to be seen, heard when "They" want to be heard. "They" have plans that humanity can't even begin to fathom, and "They" wish us harm.

This is what happened during my visit to the In and Out Diner a few weeks before Christmas. I swear to you that this is, in fact, the truth without any omissions, and this is how the events that I wit-nessed played out in their entirety.

I had taken a wrong turn off the main interstate and found that I was on a highway that was but a footnote on the map I kept in my car's glove box. I spied the sign for the In and Out as I approached and decided to take my chances there.

I was worried that the diner might be closed when I put my car in park and stepped out into the desert evening. The diner was small and shabby, and no other buildings or businesses occupied the dusty lot upon which it was built. Nothing could be seen anywhere except for a few distant lights from passing cars far off on the main interstate.

But the sign in the window read "Open" as I walked up and went to the diner's entrance, opening the door with a jingle. There was only one diesel truck with its payload attached parked to the side of the diner and a few more cars in the spots near my own. I hoped that I could make it to a motel before I fell asleep at the wheel. But I needed some information first. I was really in the middle of nowhere.

I sat down at the diner's lunch counter, and the frumpy waitress came over to hand me a menu and to say hello. "You're no truck driver, sir. What takes you past the In and Out so close to the holi-days? We've had only our regulars here tonight." She seemed friendly enough, so I gave her my story.

"I'm driving further out west to my brother's house for Christmas. He, his wife, and two daughters wanted me to visit as I haven't seen them since our mother passed away early last year."

The waitress nodded and said, "I'm sorry to hear that. I lost my own mother a few years ago, too. But my brothers and their families live in the same town as me and my husband. She was buried not far from here, in the old cemetery back when we were a mining town."

"I really don't know much about the area," I said. "I drove from out east instead of taking an airliner, as I have a phobia about flying. It's quite a drive, but I couldn't stand the long flight."

The waitress nodded again and said, "Me, I never leave. Me and my husband don't have much interest in it. Our whole family is here, so this is pretty much the world to us. But what will you have? I'm sure you didn't come in here just for some chitchat." The waitress smiled this time and took out her ballpoint pen and notepad, ready to write down my dinner order.

"I really would like some strong coffee—black, no cream or sugar. Let's start with one cup and then work our way up."

"Nothing to eat?"

"Not right now. I'll have my cup and then some directions if you don't mind."

"I'll ask the cook. He'll be able to give you better directions than I would. Like I said, I never leave."

I watched the waitress pour a mug of coffee from a pot sitting on a warmer behind the counter and made note of the one other patron, an older heavyset truck driver reading a newspaper over his finished dinner plate. He sat a few booths away from my stool at the lunch counter and made no notice of my conversation with the waitress.

She returned with my coffee mug and placed it in front of me. "You get two more refills, and then after that, you have to pay for each, which would be fifty cents. I wouldn't drink too many if I were you. You have to get to sleep tonight once you find a place to stay."

"Thank you, I just need to stay awake long enough to find a motel. Where is the cook? I would like those directions for the interstate once he is available."

The waitress leaned back against some plastic milk crates near the kitchen doors. "Oh, he'll be out soon. He's cleaning up in back. Larry over there was our last customer who ordered food and that was about an hour ago. No one might come in for the rest of the night, and we can't let the grill stay dirty."

With that, the truck driver rose from his booth and made his way past both of us, placing a rolled-up newspaper under his arm. He offered a terse good-bye to the waitress and headed out the front door, another jingle trailing behind him. I watched the man walk to his parked truck. The trucker reached his cab and then pulled himself up into its unlocked side door, starting the ignition.

"Larry comes through here about once every two weeks. He delivers for one of the major retailers in the tri-state area, so there is always something in his load that has to be at a certain place at a certain time. I think he's gonna retire soon. So many years on the road gets to a fella sooner or later."

The cab of the diesel truck turned in the parking lot in front of the diner and moved its cargo with it, advancing onto the far lane of the two-lane highway reaching past the establishment. I watched the back of the truck disappear into the distance and noted its out-of-state license plate.

"Well, it's just you and me, hon. Are you ready for another cup of straight black?"

"Yes, please. I could use one more."

This time the waitress brought the pot of coffee over to me and poured it right in front of me. "You know, people who take their coffee black are supposed to be psychopaths. Have you ever heard that before?" The waitress smirked without looking at me while the mug filled up, and then she took the pot away, returning it to the warmer behind the counter.

"My ex-wife used to tell that. One of those bogus studies someone might read about in a magazine."

"It might be true. Maybe it's more of a chicken-and-egg thing. The caffeine in the black coffee is what makes them psychopaths."

The waitress stood looking at me from in front of the kitchen doors. She was an older woman, perhaps in her sixties, wearing a few layers of aprons over a light button-down beige-colored sweater and a long skirt. Her name tag read, "Dahlia."

"I'll see what the cook is up to and get you those directions to the next motel over. Be back in a minute or two."

Dahlia went through the swinging traffic doors into the kitchen area and they closed behind her. From where I was seated, I could see the back-area ceiling florescent light fixture through the double doors' two small windows but nothing else.

I was beginning to nod off despite the two cups of coffee, but I knew I had to stay alert for my drive to the motel. I wondered what kind of fleabag or rat trap I might have to end up flopping in for the night, but I was too exhausted to care very much.

I pivoted on my stool at the counter and faced the large picture window to my left that was segmented from the right-side window by the diner's single glass-and-metal door. The windows' dull-brown aluminum blinds were drawn up on both sides and provided a good view of the highway. I could see no cars on the road, and the parking lot was vacant save for my sedan and the two parked cars that I guessed were owned by Dahlia and the cook.

The desert night was very clear, but there was nothing to be seen past the highway. Nothing appeared to have been constructed along the length of the highway on either side other than this lonesome eatery. The diner was in its own kind of oasis among the sagebrush, cactuses, and flinty hills that stretched for miles around it in every direction, without a sign of civilization other than the neglected highway.

I waited patiently while seated on my stool and swiveled around to look at the drained bottom of my coffee mug. The sheet metal counter had been wiped clean, reflecting the sterile lights running along the length of the diner's ceiling. The diner was now as silent as a tomb, and my apprehension grew, as I could not hear any sound from the back kitchen.

Nothing from Dahlia. I didn't want to barge into an employee area, as it might upset them, but at least fifteen minutes had passed without her return. I looked at my watch. Midnight was approaching quickly; Dahlia and the cook hadn't left, as their cars were in plain sight. Maybe they were out in back having a smoke before closing time?

This is where my story veers into the unexplainable. What I saw over the next several hours defies any rational interpretation. Was I dreaming due to sleepiness? I think not, unless I had a lucid dream that lasted the whole night. Even so, my own imagination could not have plunged such visions or concocted such utterances. "Their" contours are not of this world or even this reality. "Their" tones are not those made by natural vocal organs or tongues.

But what did I see? I will tell you about the first one that I met in the diner's back room.

I walked behind the counter and pushed open the leaden traffic doors, hoping to find Dahlia or the mystery cook. There was a short, unadorned hallway that was bisected by an open doorway to the unseen kitchen.

I poked my head into the kitchen and saw a cold grill framed by shelves of supplies and utensils but no waitress or chef. Mostly bare wire racks populated the rest of the space with an abbreviated alcove that was home to a steel sink and faucet. Dried dishes rested on a simple table covered in rubber sheets, forming a barrier to the freezer door at the back of the kitchen area. The kitchen had been recently washed up, but there was otherwise no indication that anyone was about the place.

I continued to believe that they were out in the back, enjoying a cigarette before returning to me with the news of my lodgings. But that is when I heard an object fall, farther down the hallway past the kitchen, followed by the characteristic sound of clanging metallic pots striking the floor and rolling.

I called out, "Dahlia? Do you need some help? I'm sorry to have come back here, but I was getting worried. I really do need to be on my way."

I turned the corner out of the kitchen and peered into the dimly lit end of the hallway. A shiny cooking pot with a black plastic handle had rolled from the part of the hall that continued to the right, resting on its side against the wall. The sound of grunting and sniffling, as if coming from a rooting pig, was audible from immediately outside of my view down that same dark passageway.

I thought, "I hope it's a dog. What else could it be?"

I made a sharp turn into the dingy ingress, and then I saw it digging through the cardboard boxes of foodstuffs that lined the wall across from the diner's back exit door. Now that I was within ten or so feet of it, I could smell and even taste the sulfurous odors being emitted from the creature's body.

How do I describe such a thing? This was the first time I had seen one of "Them." As I would find out soon enough, "They" only reveal themselves at certain times and to certain persons, but "They" are always present, always watching, always observing us. "They" may have made slips in the distant past—which then became the basis of myths and legends among humanity—but "They" have almost always been meticulously careful, only choosing to show themselves to those who are alone and isolated from the masses of mankind.

Let me attempt to describe it then. Its face was a mockery of a human face, distorted and mixed with animal-like features. Its bald, sloped head rested on its narrow shoulders with no visible neck and its pointed ears nearly met an almost impossibly wide mouth filled with serrated teeth.

The creature was hunched, standing about four feet tall, its elongated arms ending in clawed hands that hung from its seemingly nude body. Bowed, stunted legs met what looked like a vestigial tail extending from its thick backside. Its loose skin appeared rough and was a yellowish-gray color of a truly unwholesome pallor and texture.

Despite the beast's gruesome appearance, the monster had a strangely neotenous quality that reminded me of an embryo or tadpole.

When it saw me standing at the end of the hallway, it recoiled from me and shrieked. I was able to see that the creature had catlike eyes under reptilian, nictitating membranes before it flung open the exit door with its warped limbs and scurried outside.

The open exit door let in a soft light that seemed like twilight but with a diffused, purplish hue. I feared leaving the diner, but I saw no other choice. I had to try to discover what had happened to Dahlia and then report what I had seen to the authorities after I was able to reach the main interstate. I hadn't noticed a payphone in the diner, and there was no other way to communicate from our remote location.

I stepped into the open doorway and saw the alien landscape and its vista. The colors of everyday life and the nighttime desert had been replaced with an entire spectrum of purple shades.

The sky was a deep velvety purple set as a backdrop against four moons arched in a descending row across the cloudless firmament. The barren moons were large and prominent, casting their violet-colored light over low hills of plum and magenta. The fine, mauve-colored sand that extended as far as the eye could see gave off a ghostly lavender glow, highlighting flowering plants and cycads that punctuated the sand's surface. The abnormal plants themselves radiated an amethyst sheen that accentuated the moon's all-encompassing gleam, bathing the endless landscape in a perpetual blanket of incandescent illumination. It was as if reality had suddenly been turned inside out and became awash in a chromatic emendation.

I took one dip into the sand surrounding the diner's exterior from its back steps and could feel that it was solid. I made light footprints as I walked forward and spied the creature from the diner scampering off in the distance. I hastened to the front of the diner and saw that the view here was the same: sand pushing out forever in every direction with hills somewhere off in the distance. The only sound was from howling winds beyond the hills, the reverberations of which occasionally produced swirling sand at my feet.

The parking lot, cars, and the highway were gone. The diner had been uprooted, its walls and foundation dragged into another universe.

I then started to hear gibbering sounds not far from me that grew increasingly audible, multiplying in number. Weird shadows were thrown over me as I continued to survey my new world, making an irregular pattern of odd shapes from somewhere nearby. The creature's cohorts were closing in, and I had nowhere to run.

"They" started to appear, one by one or sometimes in groups of two or three. Many of the creatures bore a close resemblance to the one I first met in the diner—some were bigger, but others were even smaller. There were others that were winged, others that had many legs or arms, others that were almost amorphous and undulated across the mauve-colored sand to rest within several feet of me, faintly pulsating from an internal heartbeat. The creatures had formed a semicircle around me, blocking any advancement, with my back to the diner's front door. There was no escape.

That is when I saw their leader, the one who would explain. He strode toward me out of the desert from behind the semicircle of his minions. He was very tall and gaunt, with the same yellowish-gray skin as most of the others. His bald head was swollen in size, and his eyes were very large but nearly human, showing an intelligence that the smaller creatures appeared to lack. When he stepped inside the barrier of creatures and faced me at its edge, he spoke to me.

"Do you know why you are here?" His voice was hollow, and I could see that his thin, lipless mouth was not moving as he articulated his message. The previously constant gibbering among the creatures had subsided, and there was silence among the throng of aberrations. I could only hear the master's words in my head and nothing else; even the wind seemed to have stopped.

I was so frightened as to be almost numb. I could hear myself say, "Where am I? Where is Dahlia?"

"She is with us."

"But who are you? Have I died?" I couldn't recall dying, but I could think of no other explanation for my circumstance.

"No, you are alive. But you will have a new purpose." The leader continued, his lanky arms loose at his sides, his - to all appearances - sexless body bereft of any garments. The creature opened one of his disproportionately enormous hands and pointed a long, frail finger at my chest. "The role that Dahlia had filled will now be your role. We require an anchor through which we can see and hear outside. A living conduit so we can pass through The Veil."

"Dahlia is one of you?"

"No, she was a fleshy, as are you. But we remade her and all those before her. Her time has passed, and you are her successor."

"I can't...I don't think I can do this." I noticed that the gathering of creatures had begun to murmur, their unnatural babble now converging with the thought-speech of the leader. The doyen of the creatures lowered his index finger and said, "You have one last chance. Become one with us, or we will send you back."

The level of excitement among the crowd of monsters was noticeable. "Then send me back! I want to go back!" I was hoping for mercy even though there was no reason to expect any.

The leader's voice changed almost imperceptibly. "Then we will send you back...but not as you are. There is a price."

With that, the leader took two steps forward and grasped my head in his massive palm. The horde of monstrosities leapt in and tore at all of my limbs, stretching them with tremendous force as I was held in place. An opaque whirlwind churned around me, all feeling being stripped from my anatomy until I lost consciousness.

I awoke seated at the diner lunch counter, my head dozed over both arms that were lying crossed in front of me. I sat up as the dawn light shone into the unoccupied diner and reflected off the counter's burnished metal. I felt very weak and struggled to stand. That is when I first caught sight of myself.

I staggered to one of the picture windows to verify what I had seen in the distant reflection. That is when I saw what you see before you now.

As I mentioned, this may seem unbelievable, but it truly is what happened. I am not superstitious, nor have I ever held any thoughts about the supernatural until that night. My only hope is to warn others about "Them" before it may be too late. "They" are everywhere, even though hardly anyone even realizes it. "They" are only seen when "They" want to be seen, heard when "They" want to be heard. "They" have plans that humanity can't even begin to fathom, and "They" wish us harm.

George McKinney looked up from his seat at the doctor standing behind him without saying anything. The clinic's ward psychiatrist reached past George's left shoulder and shut off the tape recorder that rested on the table between the two men. Across from George was a decrepit old man bound in a straightjacket, slumped but still seated on a folding chair. His breathing was coarse and strained; the words that he had just finished speaking into the clinic session recorder were slurred and difficult to comprehend.

The old man wheezed as two hulking orderlies, who had been stationed at the door to the evaluation room, responded to a gesture from Dr. Leidholm and came to collect him. As they helped him to his feet, the infirmed elder seemed to flash a glimmer of recognition at George, which then quickly vanished. Hobbled and burdened with advanced age, he went back to his cell, assisted by the orderlies in his journey.

"Is it really necessary to restrain him like that? The poor fellow can barely put one foot in front of the other." George looked concerned but also uneasy; his brother, Patrick, had been missing for months, and this superannuated asylum inmate was the only potential clue to his whereabouts.

"The police consider him a suspect. He was found with your brother's wallet and car keys, but the car hasn't been recovered. Our patient also insists that he is, in fact, your brother, Patrick McKinney." Dr. Leidholm took the cassette tape from the recorder and put it into a plastic case. He marked the case's paper label with his pen and then stored the tape in his tan leather briefcase that had been kept under the examination room table.

"How would he know about my brother other than from his driver's license? He may have just found the wallet and car keys along the road where he was wandering before the sheriff picked him up. But you know, there is an eerie semblance in how that old man told his crazy story and how my brother used to speak. He was very well educated, a professor of ancient and medieval philosophy at the university level."

"We have no idea. Our John Doe has retold that fable almost word for word each time we have recorded it. The rest of the time, he has been mostly incoherent. A lot of jabbering about 'They' and 'Them.' He thinks 'They' come to visit him in his cell.

"We did extract something from his person that is highly unusual, however, something that could almost lend credence to his tale if it wasn't so fantastic."

"And what is that? May I see it?"

Dr. Leidholm opened his briefcase yet again and presented George with a transparent laboratory vial that was capped at its top. The vial was half filled with very fine, purplish sand.

"The sand was in his shoes, pants pockets, and even what remains of the old man's hair when he was brought into the clinic by the sheriff's department for evaluation. We first noticed the stuff when an orderly removed his loafers."

George took the flask from the doctor and held it up before himself. The tiny grains in the glass tube emanated an unearthly purple luster, sparkling with an eternal fire.

STELLA

"I won't be gone for long—three months at the most. David and I want to complete our collection and then make one final donation to the museum. You worry too much, Chad. Really, you do."

Judith stood in front of a large crate that was carefully packed with boxes. She held an ornate vase in the shape of a man's head, wrapped it in brown paper, and then slid the vase into a thick, rectangular cardboard box, before placing the item inside the crate among the other boxes. The crate was marked "FRAGILE" in blocky black letters and was one of a number of identical crates in the otherwise empty room.

Chad continued his dialogue. "It's just that the country isn't safe right now, with everything that's been happening there politically. Americans have been murdered or worse; the U.S. embassy has even issued a travel advisory. It's a risk I wouldn't take, especially during the summer months. That's when the vultures are out, looking for tourists."

"We are not tourists." Judith paused her work and turned toward her brother. "We are archeologists—but amateur ones."

"Patrons of the arts."

"Yes, exactly."

"Armed gunmen wouldn't be impressed. They would want your cash, not your knowledge of the region's indigenous artwork."

Judith put her hand on a hip and rolled her eyes—a mannerism typical of hers that she had never outgrown, even in middle age.

"I only want my big sister to be safe. It's not like David is going to save you if you are in bind."

Judith became animated. "Chad, David is a good man! It's just that he's so…" Judith's voice trailed off, and she looked away from Chad. "We will be with paid guides and an excavation crew, so it won't be just the two of us. We'll be fine, I promise." She finished wrapping the last few artifacts in their boxes and then stowed them away.

"Our flight leaves on Sunday, and we'll be back by mid-August, worst-case scenario. I'll call you if anything changes. The exhibit at the metropolitan museum is in March, so the pieces have to be donated, received by the museum staff, and then made ready for presentation soon."

Judith walked with Chad to the front door of her home and opened it for him. Chad stepped out of the foyer and then turned to face Judith. "Are you going to stay at that monastery with the nuns you told me about after your last trip?"

"Yes, Reverend Mother Magdalena said that we could stay at the monastery and use it as our base—in exchange for a not-so-modest donation, of course. Only me and David, however, not our guides or crew.

"The monastery is very high up in the mountains, and it is the closest settlement to the dig site. If we didn't use the monastery as our staging area, we would either have to camp with the crew or make the trip back to town every evening if the Reverend Mother hadn't given us permission. I really don't savor the idea of sleeping in a tent next to some of our guides."

Chad grimaced slightly and then put his hand on his sister's shoulder. "Be safe. I will want to hear about your adventures when you get back."

That was the last time that Chad had seen Judith. Chad watched his wife put their remaining bags on the curb pavement in front of the double doors of the city airport's main entrance.

Chad looked up and down the car lanes that stretched past the airport's arrival and departure area. "Look for the car sent by the hotel. The cabbies at the airport might not be the real deal."

"I have everything," Sarah said. "No lost luggage."

Chad pushed his sunglasses further up the bridge of his nose as his skin was slightly damp from perspiration. "We should be at the hotel in few hours. We can get a good night's sleep and then take care of matters. We'll hire a driver to take us as close to Mother Magdalena's monastery as we can get by vehicle. A local guide will be able to take us the rest of the way."

Chad and Sarah sat in the back seat of the air-conditioned SUV as the driver navigated the busy highway downtown. The SUV came to a halt behind a long line of traffic near the exit to the downtown plaza. "This is one of the best hotels in the city." The driver spoke English very clearly, without a pronounced accent. "Close to both the Marriott and the Radisson. And about a ten-minute walk to Calle de las Fuentes from the hotel."

Sarah lay on the hotel bed but didn't disturb the linen cover. "Do you want to go for a walk downtown before we call it a night? It's much cooler now, and a walk would help us relax after that flight."

Chad took off his watch, placing it on the large dresser at the foot of the bed and sat down in front of Sarah. "I really can't relax until we know more. I'm sorry to be so tense, but there is still a chance we can find out something about Judith."

"Both of them have been missing for months. I'm sorry, Chad, but I don't think we are going to find them here. There were no bodies, no one knows what happened. All anyone has to go on is what that little girl might have seen, and she isn't talking."

"Judith was so excited that final time I spoke to her over the phone. She and David were going to bring the girl back with them and legally adopt her. They had never had any kids of their own, and Judith saw this as her chance to be a mother."

Sarah rested her head in the palm of her arched arm and continued, "Why was Judith so interested in this country? I can understand the art collection, but what is it about this place that's so compelling? She and David spent so much time here amassing those artifacts for the museum, but what else was in it for them?"

Chad was very tall, with sandy-blond hair and an athletic build. He stood out very sharply in contrast to the local people, as did Sarah. Chad and Sarah had even been mistaken for fraternal twins on a number of occasions.

Chad lay across from Sarah and then rolled over on his back, with his face toward the ceiling. "Judith never felt comfortable at home. She really needed to get out and explore…see the world.

"Judith studied art history in college and became fascinated with what the native people had created in this region. She learned the language and kept returning. The excavation site they were working on was sponsored by the museum, but our family had put up the funding for most of the project."

Chad stood up from the bed and walked to the balcony window, taking in the view of the city at night. "The girl is there waiting for us. Reverend Mother Magdalena said that she would like us to at least meet her. The girl has no family, and nothing is really known about her. But she was the last person who saw Judith and David alive."

Reverend Mother Magdalena strode down the long columnated pathway connecting the brightly painted stucco buildings of the monastery. The Reverend Mother reached the front gates of the courtyard, where Chad and Sarah were waiting to meet her.

"I'm glad that you are here. I am so sorry about Judith and her husband. The police investigated for several months but were unable to make very much progress."

Chad tried to appear comfortable and said, "Yesterday we met with the detective assigned to the case. He explained how the investigation went and apologized for not being able to find anything at all. No evidence of what had happened. He assured me that such a case is highly irregular and that the police had made their best effort."

Chad had only seen the Reverend Mother before in a few photographs brought back by Judith after her penultimate trip. Mother Magdalena was not much older than Judith and had sharp, angular facial features set against the neatly pressed, flowing white coif of her nun's habit.

"*Hacer de hablas español?* It is all right if you don't. I studied in the United States for a number of years, but I don't have to use English all that often. I am 'rusty,' as you would say."

Chad smiled apologetically. "No, neither of us have a foreign language, I'm sorry to tell you. Judith was the cosmopolitan one of the two siblings."

"All right, then; I think you should meet Stella. She is in her room near the back of the monastery."

The expansive courtyard of the monastery was lined with olive trees along its stone and adobe walls that shielded its buildings from the outside. The nuns lived in isolation from the nearby communities farther down the mountain range, with the exception of the monastery's groundskeepers and handymen who maintained the buildings. These men were members of the local indigenous populations but could converse with the sisters in Spanish.

Mother Magdalena brought Chad and Sarah down a long hall after reentering the monastery that ended with a simple wooden door to their left, featuring a tarnished bronze knob.

"This was a storage room before we set up Stella in here." Mother Magdalena made one quick knock and then opened the door to a plain whitewashed room that had only a cot and a clothes dresser as furniture. A young girl of about ten years old was sitting on the bed, looking out of a solitary window at the monastery grounds. She wore a basic white cotton tunic and was barefoot.

"Stella, *familia de Judith está aquí.*" The girl turned to face the visitors but did not move from her spot. She had large, almond-shaped black eyes with an elongated face and dark-brown skin.

"Stella speaks no English at all but also no Spanish. She has learned a little Spanish since staying at the monastery but doesn't speak it. Stella does know bits of the local language, but her pronunciation is very odd, almost archaic."

Chad walked toward the cot and crouched down next to the motionless girl. "Stella, I'm Chad. I'm Judith's brother." Stella looked at him silently and then turned away, back toward observing the outside window.

"After David and Judith found Stella, she didn't speak, no matter what we tried. We thought that she might be mute. Then one of our groundskeepers spoke to her in his indigenous dialect, and she answered him.

"She's perfectly healthy, though; we had a doctor examine her, and he could find no evidence of physical trauma. I think she will start speaking again in time and then tell us her story. But let us leave Stella for now. I will introduce you to Sister Claudia."

Mother Magdalena and Chad filed out of the small room, and Sarah followed, turning around once to glance at Stella. Stella turned her head away from the window again and gave Sarah an expressionless stare as the door closed behind them.

Sister Claudia walked up the steep path in front of Chad and Sarah that led along the periphery of the jungle canopy. The sister wore clothes suitable to making the climb in the mountains nearby the monastery but still retained a nun's short coif that hid most of her glossy black hair. When they had hiked to what seemed to be the top, she pointed to a suspension bridge in the distance that had become clearly defined.

"The Reverend Mother asked me to show you the excavation site as—other than herself—I can speak your language. I read Theology at Oxford for two years, so maybe not quite *your* language. I am also young enough to make the climb without too much trouble."

The sister smiled at both of them when she stopped near the suspension bridge for a rest. Chad paused and then looked over at Sarah to make sure she was going to be able to reach the bridge.

"The workers refurbished the bridge before the excavation started last spring. They reinforced the planks and made sure that everything was secure, as it was going to get a lot of use. Once we get to the other side, the site is a quick climb down—maybe thirty minutes."

"Oh, is that all?" Sarah stopped and breathed slowly, bending forward with her hands on her knees. "I need to take a drink from my water bottle. I'll catch up if you want to keep going." The atmosphere was very thin, and Sarah's labored efforts punctuated the new environment the couple was experiencing.

Chad looked out over the vista and could see no visible structures. The monastery was obscured by the canopy that they had now passed since reaching the mountain's skyline.

Chad said, "C'mon, honey, you can make it. It's not much farther."

Sister Claudia led them into a shallow, circular quarry that terminated at the side of the mountain. There were still canvas tents and crates scattered around the site, as all supplies had not been collected in anticipation of the possibility that work might resume in the near future.

"The workers and your sister had already procured some substantial finds, but only the surface has been scratched so far. What relics they had excavated and dusted are being kept in storage at the monastery. Your sister and the guides seemed to think that this place was once a temple to an indigenous deity, an animal god of some sort."

Sister Claudia shaded her eyes with a hand and motioned around them with her free one in a sweeping gesture. "There are dozens of stone statues that have become almost completely submerged in the landscape and ring the mountains for miles in an elliptical pattern. The buried temple is at the exact center of the ellipse. That is how the team found this place and then decided where to start excavating.

"There are no mentions of this religious site in any oral tradition among the natives or anything else that might point to its existence. The temple could even predate human settlement in this area."

The opening in the side of the mountain's surface had been delved by the excavation crew using a mole-drilling machine, but only the outer plaza of the structure was visible from the quarry. The tunneled opening revealed a stone-tiled floor partially covered in debris, but nothing else was perceptible from the outside.

"The temple had been built into the contours of the mountain itself and then sealed by an avalanche, possibly on purpose."

Chad and Sarah turned and looked at each other, and then Sarah sat down on a nearby crate covered in a canvas sheet. Chad started to wander off by himself around the quarry, kicking loose stones with his foot.

Sarah said, "Why did the authorities agree to allow Judith and the museum to work on this dig? These kinds of sites could produce national treasures worth millions."

"Our government didn't have the money for this kind of project, but Chad's sister and the museum did. All the artifacts which have been excavated from the site will be returned to our country after being exhibited at the museum for an agreed-upon amount of time."

Sister Claudia walked closer to the temple's roped threshold and peered into the tenebrous opening, the interior of which was barely discernible now due to the rain clouds forming overhead.

"The greater temple beyond the surrounding court perimeter has yet to be breached, from my understanding. I can't even tell you what is past there. On the far side of the dig site is a plateau that overlooks the rain forest. That is where two of the workers first found Stella. Let me show you."

Chad stood at the edge of the flat rock cliff and saw below that the deep valley's leafy cover spread until the next mountain range in the inaccessible distance. Sister Claudia was nearby on a lower ledge that connected to the mountain via a narrow trial that extended all the way down into the heart of the rain forest.

"The men had been working at the site and were caught in a torrential rain that suddenly appeared during the afternoon. The rain went on for hours but dissipated before the evening. Then someone noticed a tiny figure sitting on this ledge in the twilight." Sister Claudia knelt down to touch the reddish stone surface of the cliff.

"Stella was alone and naked, sitting with her arms around her knees. The rock was slick from the downpour, but she would not move. One of the crew members ran to the monastery to fetch Judith, hoping Stella wouldn't be afraid of a woman. Judith was able to get Stella to leave her perch, and she has been at the monastery since that night.

The sisters named her Stella, as she couldn't give us her birth name. Stella means 'star' in classical Latin, as she was found under a very clear, starry sky after the rain. Judith didn't want to change it."

Chad had joined Sister Claudia on the lower cliff and stood next to her. "Do you know any more about the night that Judith and David disappeared? The detective told us they had left the monastery grounds without letting anyone know and then never came back. Stella was found wandering outside in the jungle nearby, so the police supposed that she had most likely been with Judith and David when they vanished, or at least initially."

Sister Claudia looked right at Chad and drew closer to him. She said, "What else did the detective tell you about Stella?"

"Nothing. He said that she was their only probable witness, but she either can't or won't say what she might have seen."

Her voice lowered, and the nun's tone changed to one of trepidation. "I was the one who found Stella outside during the search. Her cotton tunic was badly torn and soiled, but there was not a mark on her. It was almost as if she had been dragged across the jungle floor without so much as a scratch."

"All of it is here, in the four biggest crates, with English-language script on the outside." Mother Magdalena raised one of the tarp covers to show Chad and Sarah the name of the museum where the artifacts would be added to the collection that had already been donated by Judith.

"Customs know that these items are coming, so they will be shipped out by sea around the same time that your flight leaves. The museum staff is ready to receive them."

"Thank you. I appreciate what you did for Judith and David while they were here. I will let you know if the case is ever reopened in light of new information."

"You're welcome, Mr. Isaac. Judith truly loved this country—almost as much as she loved Stella."

"So what will happen to Stella?" Sarah stood next to Mother Magdalena and crossed her arms. "Will she be raised as a nun in training?"

Mother Magdalena laughed and said, "Oh no, we can't rear children here. The monastery is a place for religious contemplation, not a nursery."

Sarah continued, saying, "Where will Stella go then? She has already been with the sisters for months."

Mother Magdalena became serious and gestured to the folding chairs situated near the crates. "Please sit down."

Chad and Sarah seated themselves, and Mother Magdalena sat across from them. She took one of Sarah's hands in both of hers. "I would like you and Chad to adopt Stella—as Judith and David had planned."

Chad was taken aback and sat up abruptly. "We can't, Mother Magdalena. Even if we could, there is all the government red tape and the visa to consider. I have to return to my law practice by next week."

"Everything is ready. I have already made all the arrangements with child services and immigration. You will just have to complete the process once you return to the States. If you don't adopt Stella, she will end up in a government-run orphanage. We can't keep her."

Sarah touched Chad's shoulder. "Let's please talk this over. Judith would have wanted this." Chad thought back to their initial meeting with Stella and how cold she had seemed when they had entered her bedroom and tried to greet her.

Stella sat in the back seat of their convertible sports car, with her fine, chin-length black hair blowing around her face. Sarah occupied the passenger seat next to Chad as he drove them from the international airport, paging through her travel guide with pictures of indigenous artwork. Objects from the same period illustrated in Sarah's guidebook had followed them on their trip home and would soon be on display to the public.

Chad looked into the rearview mirror and was able to see Stella briefly before returning to focus on the road home. Stella had noticeably warmed to the couple following their departure from the remote monastery, and she turned her head to look at them in the front seat, smiling faintly. Chad remarked to himself how similar the girl appeared to the ancient people depicted on the mountain temple's mosaic art. The local inhabitants were the direct descendants of the civilization that had existed in the region for thousands of years before European settlement.

Chad drove past palm trees on the highway and then up long stretches of hillside road until reaching the sparsely populated woodland exurbs outside the metropolitan city. Chad made an hour-long commute to his office and then back again every workday, just for the opportunity to live in relative isolation and privacy. The red sun dipped over the horizon as the car sped past the homes dotting the scenery, and the evening air became chill, as spring had not yet turned into summer in the desert.

"What's that in the driveway, darling?" Sarah had put her book down into her lap as they approached their home and leaned over the side door of the car from her seat. "It looks like a tarantula," Chad replied. "One of the orange striped kind. They come into the yard sometimes from the thick cluster of trees behind the house. Too bad we don't have any neighbors to attract them elsewhere."

Sarah continued to watch the lurking spider from the car's passenger seat. "Be careful when we step out of the car. Keep an eye on that thing so it doesn't get too close."

Chad smiled without looking at Sarah. "We won't have to worry about it in a minute."

Sarah looked over at Chad and said, "Why? That bug is almost the size of a small kitten." Sarah again leaned out over the side door as Chad pulled their car into the semicircle driveway in front of their two-story stucco residence. Chad drove over the spider from which a detectable crunch was heard as the tire rolled over it.

Stella sat up in the back seat immediately and was very still. Her eyes were wide, and she had a disconcerted expression on her face. Chad continued to drive the car around the semicircle and then opened the automatic garage door, parking their car inside. Stella remained stationary in the back seat until Chad opened the side door of the convertible and looked down at her. Stella then turned to look up at Chad and gave him a piercing glare that made him take one step back.

Chad walked away from the car and out of the open garage door. He said, "Sarah, can you take Stella inside? I am going to clean off the driveway with a hose before we unpack."

Sarah switched ears and continued to speak into the cordless phone. "No, Stella has been sleeping very well for weeks. But she hardly ever speaks—even now. She knows some English words for food and a few other things, but we can't get her to really talk to us. I want to bring Stella to a speech therapist after we get settled in and the museum runs our exhibition.

"OK. Please call me next week before we stop into social services. I know there is some more paperwork we have to go over before the formal adoption procedure begins in earnest."

Sarah hung up the phone and then looked at Chad who was standing facing her. "You don't have to come with me the first few times, but we are going to need your signature on everything, probably next month."

Chad walked behind Sarah and then wrapped his arms around her shoulders, pressing his face against the side of her head. "Of course, I want to be as involved with the adoption as much as necessary, but I can't miss any more work. I have to go to trial next week, so that means more long hours with the litigation team and the requisite face time at the office. I couldn't even drop everything when Judith first went missing, as I was elbow deep at the firm. The consulate assured me that she would turn up soon, but…"

Sarah turned around on the kitchen stool and hugged Chad underneath his arms, placing her head on his chest. "Stella is all we have left of Judith. I really want us to be good parents to our girl. We will be a family."

Chad tapped away at the keyboard, drafting a long e-mail response to the firm partner that had been assigned to work with his team. He had eaten dinner at the office and was preparing to leave for home before it became a late-night drive. The desk phone rang even though it was after business hours, and Chad picked up the call.

"Oh, Mr. Isaac, I'm sorry. I was expecting to go to your voice mail. This is Jared Scott, the curator for Judith's collection at the metropolitan museum. Your sister and I were close friends, but you and I have never met in person." The museum curator spoke with precise diction, befitting that of a scholar of antiquity.

Chad replied, "Good to make your acquaintance, Mr. Scott. I appreciate the efforts you have made on behalf of Judith's donated pieces. Sarah and I are looking forward to the opening day of the exhibit. What is the tentative date as of now?"

"We have rescheduled the exhibit for a few months from now, during the first week of August. I was calling to inform you that all the items in your shipment have been catalogued and are now being prepared for display. The pieces are of a greater rarity than even we had anticipated, with some highly unusual pictographs on the temple pottery and mosaics recovered at the site."

Chad leaned back in his black leather office chair and asked, "How so? Sarah and I never saw what was boxed up in those four crates that were shipped back. The excavation crew had already prepared the shipment after work on the site had ceased."

"Mr. Isaac, the usual sacred animal spirits such as the puma, the snake, and the condor are entirely missing from the site's pictographic imagery. Instead, there are spiders on everything. We have never seen anything like this before."

"A temple to spiders? I don't know much about the country's old religions, but that sounds like a cult I wouldn't want to be a part of. Who would build a temple to some spider god?"

"The construction at the site was also not entirely a temple. From the narrative told on the mosaics we have examined, the site was not only a place of worship, Mr. Isaac. The temple at Pucahirca is a burial chamber for the victims of human sacrifice."

Chad drove home as a steady rain washed across his windshield, which was cleared away by the dull squeak of the windshield wipers swiping in unison. The car's headlights illuminated the early evening as Chad turned off the highway and drove down the two-lane road toward their hillside home.

Chad parked outside in the semicircle driveway and saw that the house was completely dark. The evening was humid after the rain had turned into a drizzle, announcing the first days of the summer months. He opened the front door and immediately noticed that the air conditioning had been shut off.

"I hope this isn't a prank," Chad called out into the kitchen from the hallway, "because it's not funny." He attempted to flip the light switch at the end of the hall, but the power was out.

Chad fumbled around in the dark kitchen and found a flashlight in the first drawer next to the stove. He looked in his and Sarah's bedroom and then in Stella's bedroom, but both were empty. He walked outside and into their backyard, noticing one of Stella's leather sandals lying in the grass near the path leading to the wooded area behind the house.

Chad picked up the sandal before continuing into the nighttime forest. The trees were very tall with hanging branches reaching out toward each other, forming a shelter from the rain and also from sunlight during the day. He continued along the path until he found Stella's other sandal and some of her clothes that had been stained with what seemed to be a pungent-smelling discharge.

Chad worried that his wife and adopted daughter might have been murdered by intruders. He called around him into the forest, "Sarah? Stella? I am going back for the police unless you come out now."

Chad heard a rustling sound close by and shone his flashlight onto the spot from which the noise emanated. He saw a man-sized cocoon suspended from the trees in the forest clearing, with the bottom of the webbed figure inches above the ground. Chad aimed his flashlight at the figure's head that pointed toward the woods' floor and saw that it was Sarah.

Sarah's face was wrapped in a thin webbing, but her eyes, nose, and mouth were partially exposed. "Oh my God...Sarah," Chad whispered.

Chad crawled next to her, and Sarah began wheezing in an attempt to speak. He put his ear next to Sarah's mouth, and she let out a barely audible, "Kill me."

Tears ran down his face as he attempted to pull at the sticky webs and free his wife. From above in the trees' canopy, a giant brown spider the size of a horse lowered itself onto the disturbed soil behind Sarah's cocoon prison. As Chad pivoted to run away, the last thing he felt was the monstrous body slam into his back.

ABOUT THE AUTHOR

An early student of philosophy and pulp literature, James Dermond was an avid reader of great (or, at least, entertaining) books. As James's interests evolved, he slowly gravitated towards writing and now writes full time.

Doorways to the Unseen: 6 Tales of Terror and Suspense is James's first book in what will be a horror short story series of the same name. There will be many more installments in this series, as well as other books, to come.

To sign up for free eBooks and other future giveaways, please subscribe to James Dermond's author website here:

www.jamesdermond.com

James Dermond's Amazon Author Page
https://www.amazon.com/James-Dermond/e/
B01M1S54YP

James Dermond's Goodreads Author Page
https://www.goodreads.com/author/show/15862747.
James_Dermond

James Dermond on Facebook
https://www.facebook.com/JamesDermondAuthor/

James Dermond on Twitter
https://twitter.com/JamesDermond